BLURB

The Pucker-Up Pact

My first year playing center for the brand-new AHL team, and things are off to a disastrous start.

After losing my temper with the refs in front of a fan-filled arena, my coach devises a plan to "make me more likable."

It's a horrible plan that isn't going to work.

He wants me to pretend to date a famous singer in hopes that her fans will become my fans.

The last thing I want to do is date, pretend to date, or think about dating. Who has time for that when I have hockey games to win? When my coach forces me to pose for a publicity photo with this woman, I vow to get it over with as quickly as possible. But she has other plans for me. With her ebony hair, mischievous smile, the unhinged female edges her way into my heart. When the magnetism between us explodes, it's game over. Just when I think

I'm ready to let Sophie melt my heart, I uncover a devastating secret that changes everything.

The Pucker-Up Pact is a grumpy sunshine, revenge fake-dating, sweet romantic comedy with a HEA.

Instant chemistry Revenge Fake Dating Forced Proximity She's mine vibes

One

Axl Erikson

Thirty seconds.

That's all the ticks the giant overhead digital clock has left, and the crowd chants down each digit, growing louder as the numbers decrease. I skate down the rink with precision speed, smoking past their lumbering defensemen, and I wait for our winger, Noah, to bring the puck over the blue line.

My heart pounds to the rhythm of the countdown, slamming against my rib cage with each second lost. I've been waiting for this shot all game.

I'm two goals in.

One more and it's not only my first hat trick of the season but, more crucially, it's the tying goal, sending us into overtime.

Their goalie glances at me, his charcoal eyes pinning on me with the kind of glare that leaves the taste of blood on my lips. I take an easy breath and swipe my tongue over my bottom lip, hydrating it.

I'm not afraid of anything. I've been training for this moment my entire life.

"You got this, Axl," I whisper under my breath as I take off with force, rerouting myself to the back of the net to get open.

"Twenty-five!" the crowd screams, and I have eyes on the puck smoothly bouncing back and forth off Noah's stick. Even though I'm open, Noah is encapsulated with the other team, causing him to slow his speed as he fights to protect the puck. Noah's a ninja on skates but he's short, which makes him an easy target.

If he could get me the puck, it's an easy shot to the goal from here.

I didn't get this far in my career because it is easy.

Who am I kidding?

It's never easy.

I need to get closer to Noah.

"Twenty-two," the crowd hollers, pumping my chest full of the adrenaline I need to swoop back around the net at full speed. And because nothing ever goes according to plan, I slip, swiftly catching my fall with my free arm. I manage to right myself as I skid until my skate blade scrapes off a layer of ice, spraying the player next to me. I'm quickly blocked from moving any closer to Noah, and the crowd becomes unhinged. "Fifteen!"

Panic seeds in my chest as I scan the rink. Noah rounds the corner of the rink, miraculously keeping the puck, the other team's defense at his heels. His skating skills could easily land him some circus on ice if this hockey thing doesn't work out. He zigs and he zags, like he's on the basketball court, all while maintaining the puck.

"Twelve," the countdown chant rumbles in the arena, and my heart rockets into overtime speed. I can get open, but Noah is covered well.

My gaze snags on their number thirteen. He's skating backwards, positioned in front of Noah. He's enormous, the size of a Mini Cooper. There's no way around him. I'm not superstitious, but I've always had a thing against the number thirteen.

Now I also have a thing against Mini Coopers.

"Ten!" The thunderous word echoes around the arena.

My lip snarls, and I make up my mind. Crouching, I dig in with my skates and rocket across the ice, eyes lasered on the black disk. As Noah glides around the back of the goal, he cuts the corner too sharply and practically lays on the ice, but he manages to stay on his skates. There's a small gap behind unlucky-number thirteen and if I can get through it, I'll be wide open for a shot at the net. I skate hard and lunge forward right as Mini Cooper slides over and trips on my stick. He's so huge, his fall makes it look like I took out half the team, and the whistle slices the air.

I freeze, searching for the ref as he makes the call.

Two-minute penalty for tripping?

He jumped on my stick!

Anger fumes up my chest and bleeps out my throat. "Are you blind?" I jerk my hand toward the ref. "He crashed into me!"

The crowd erupts in rumbles. Feet pound on stands and boos reverberate off the walls.

"That wasn't my fault!" I scream again, my free arm flying all around me in animation. My eyes hitch on Coach Carlson, whose eyes are sprouting blood-red veins that seem to pulse all the words he isn't saying as he angrily motions me to the box. It's a two-minute penalty, but worse than that, the game is essentially over. Fury courses my veins as I fight the urge to chuck my stick at the ref, and I spin around and skate to the penalty box.

Some days I hate this game.

As I jump in the box, the crowd erupts, but I don't even glance behind me.

I know all the cameras are on me. They have it out for me, as I've made a bit of a name for myself for harassing refs. Not that it was my plan. I can't help that they are ignorant. Coach has given me more than one warning about keeping my mouth shut. Somedays, I don't think this career is worth it. Between the extensive travel, the social media bullying, and the constant physical abuse of my body, I'm getting sick of it.

I spit out my mouthguard, swipe my tongue over my front teeth, and fight with all my might not to run my mouth at that stupid ref.

Stupid.

Two

Sophie Summers

"Oh, babe, I'm sorry your ankle is bugging you again." My voice laces with empathy as I tuck my phone between my shoulder and ear to ever-so-quietly not give any clues that I'm shutting a car door. I wave as the taxi driver darts back into the Thursday night New York traffic. My smile only grows larger as I pivot to cross Park Avenue to Rocco's apartment. It's his twenty-sixth birthday, and I'm supposed to be on my tour bus headed to Minneapolis for the last stop on my concert tour, but I couldn't miss his birthday. He's in the middle of his NFL season and can't get away, and I'm not okay with missing his birthday. He's the love of my life, and I want to be the person who is beside him on his special day. "Did you get hurt in practice?"

"Yeah, it's been sore all week, but I felt something give while I was running. I'm meeting the team's physical therapist. He's going to help me stretch it out and wrap it. I'm sure it will be better after I rest for a night."

"I hate that you aren't feeling well on your birthday. You should be out celebrating." My boots click out a steady rhythm, and I adjust the bags on my arms. One package is his gift, a new Rolex wrapped in a handwritten love note expressing all the ways he makes my life better. The other bag is an overnight bag with everything I need to get ready for our dinner reservations. I reserved the entire private rooftop at his favorite restaurant, and I had my favorite designer custom make a special dress for the occasion. Black satin all the way down to my toes with a classy high collar that opens to a V in the back. Rocco always told me one of the things he loves about me is the way I dress classy and not trashy, like most of the women in the clubs. It's just the way I am, never feeling comfortable showing lots of bare skin. Not to mention that after we started dating, I realized that he tends to have a jealous side when he thinks other guys are looking at me. I've learned to not provoke it by overdoing my outfits.

"Nah, you know how I am," he reassures me. "I'm not one to make a big deal about my birthday. If I can't spend the day with you, I'd rather stay home. We'll go out this weekend, and by then I'll be back to normal." His voice muffles and I don't hear what he says before he comes back clear. "Soph, the therapist is ready for me. I'll call you later. Okay?"

"Sounds good."

"Love you." His soft goodbye cushions my heart.

"Love you, too." I don't fight the enormous smile on my face as I end the call and turn to greet Rocco's door attendant. I'm here so much we are on a first name basis. "Good evening, Ben. How are you?"

His blue eyes pass over me and he doesn't bend a lip upward. "What are you doing here, Soph?"

Laughing off his surprise, I give him a mischievous smile, so proud am I of my sneaky surprise. "I know, I'm supposed to be on a bus, but don't worry, I didn't cancel my tour. My pilot will fly me out first thing in the morning. I have it all planned out. If I leave by seven, I'll beat my tour crew."

"No." He steps in front of the door, and his head wags side to side. "You can't go upstairs."

"I know he's not home," I rush to explain. "He's getting therapy, but if you would please sneak me up before he gets home, I'm dying to surprise him. He has no idea I'm here. It's the best surprise I could think of for his birthday."

"Soph . . ." His voice is steady but softens as he pulls out his phone, holding out the screen for me to see while scrolling down to his door camera app. "He is home, and he has company."

"Oh." Tilting my head to the side, I rewind Rocco's words, not paying an ounce of attention to what Ben has on his phone. "Maybe the therapist met him here? I can't remember exactly what he said, but it's fine if I don't beat him—" My voice drops off and ice rips through my veins, instantly making me ill, and I want to throw up.

Ben has the door camera app open, and he has rewound it in front of me to show Rocco walking through the door with a blonde woman I don't recognize, wearing a dress that I would never call classy. Their arms are wrapped around each other, and there's not a slice of air between their bodies.

"This was fifteen minutes ago," Ben adds as he scrolls back on the camera app some more. "But I can show you that she's been here all week, and trust me, if I were you, I would not go up there."

"It must be a mistake. A friend?"

"Technically, she's the team's new social media expert, but if you ask me, she's just a groupie. I wouldn't doubt she's dating more than one of the guys."

"Dating?" The word rings in my ears and I diagnose how *off* that sounds. A lump bulges in my throat, swelling even after I swallow to try to force it down. "He's dating her?"

"They haven't been discreet, if you know what I mean. I can show you more footage, but trust me, you don't want to see it." He pushes the phone back toward me, and a shadow of two figures pushed together in a lip lock flashes before me.

I turn my head away as my voice cracks, "Why are you doing this?"

"I would have called you, but I didn't want to ruin your focus on your tour. I knew the tour was ending after this week, and you deserve to have that success." His cobalt eyes spiral pity at me, and my throat dries as reality sinks in. This is not a joke. Even if this woman is a friend, he's not where he said he was just two seconds earlier . . . at the arena getting physical therapy from the *male* team therapist.

"I have to talk to him." My weakened voice floats out. "I need verification. He needs to tell me to my face that he lied."

"He's not worth it." Ben takes a giant step back and leans against the door, securing it even more.

I'm not a violent person. There's no way I'd bust through it, but his insistence on keeping me out puts my heart on full alarm. "It's not the first time, is it?"

Ben's gaze skirts to the side, and he lowers his voice. "You'd better go unless you want this on camera. There's paparazzi coming this way. Don't give them the satisfaction of seeing your disgust."

Disgust? I want to blurt out. I'm not disgusted at all. I'm gut punched. My heart is pummeled as everything I believed to be true and good has been ripped from me in two minutes. I feel ambushed. I simply want to see Rocco to confirm that this is all a lie, but at the same time, there's no reason Ben would lie to me about this. We've been friends since Rocco and I started dating, which has been over a year now. "Tell me when the infidelity started," I squeak out, still trying to find the place in my memory of something I did wrong.

Was there some way I could have caused this?

Maybe I could still fix it.

I've been on the road an awful lot, even missing some of his games.

"I only discovered it recently, since your last trip."

"Two weeks." I breathe out, one eye tracing the paparazzi coming down the sidewalk. I pull my baseball cap down, concealing my eyes, as I try to convince myself that two weeks isn't that long.

He can't possibly *love* this woman.

Not how he loves me.

It's just a mistake.

We could work on it.

I'm willing to try if he's honest and comes clean.

"I'm sorry, but that particular woman has been here all week, and the paparazzi already suspects something is up with Rocco. They'll get a photo sooner or later, and it might be best if you're not in it." He nods to the left, away from the oncoming reporter. "You need to leave now."

My hands fly to the bill of my cap, shielding the sides of my face as my cheeks rage in overwhelm and heartbreak. My knees buckle, and moving is not an option. My romance with Rocco flashes before my eyes, and I'm mourning all the romantic dinners, private vacations, and never-ending phone conversations. I can't walk away from that, even if my legs could move.

"You need to leave before you cause a scene." Ben's voice grows in urgency, but it's too late. Not one or two, but a barrage of phone cameras point at me now. One is from the nearest paparazzi, another is from some guy who popped up across the street, and more are from down the block. I'm surrounded, and I can't even defend myself.

I'm melting.

But I'm not.

I'm clearly still standing out in the open for all to take photos of. Could I please melt?

"For Pete's sake, don't just stand there." Ben whips the front door open, and yells, "Get inside." I slip inside, and Ben follows on my heels. Marching me to the closest door, which happens to be the mailroom, he says, "You can hide in here, and I'll get a car to come around the back."

As he pivots to return to his post, I call out, "I'm sorry. I froze."

"It's okay." He tuns back with a sympathetic look on his face. "You're the one who is owed an apology."

Suddenly, I'm in a flashback.

At sixteen years old, I promised myself I was going for everything everyone told me I couldn't have.

They said I couldn't have fame.

I took the hard road, counting each small success as a win, and eventually, I got it.

They scoffed and said my fame was fleeting, and that I'd need a job to build real wealth.

I was smart, investing in myself, and by not wasting even a dime I've accumulated a lot of wealth over the years.

Then they said that even if I could do all that, I would never be able to both work that hard and find true love.

They got me on that one. A single hot tear slips out of my eye, and I let it glide all the way down my cheek.

I guess they were right.

Three

Axl

It's a frigid morning, and my brand-new financed Dodge Ram crawls to a stop in the shadowy parking lot at the Mapleton, Vermont, arena two hours before practice is scheduled.

I've got work to do if I want to get moved up to the NHL.

This is how I get ahead.

I've always done it this way.

If everyone else practices at eight, I begin at six.

If everyone else goes out to celebrate right after a game win, I go back to the rink and start over, prepping for the next game. I never let my game slide.

Killing the engine, I jump out of the truck and briskly walk to the front entrance, where the janitor has left the door unlocked for me. Small towns are nice like that. That's one good thing about playing for this brand-new AHL team—that hardly anybody knows exists yet, but that's beside the point—it's in a small town, and it's been an easy adjustment. The salary is hardly any-thing to brag about. The optimist in me calls this mid-five-figure salary, one which leaves lots of room for upward growth. It's only my first year out of college, and I'm lucky I get to play at all.

Most of the lights are dim, but it's bright enough I don't get the creeps walking through this place when it's empty. These early mornings alone on the ice rejuvenate my spirit, reminding me why I push myself so hard. There's nothing that I'm running from, but I have one of those personalities where I like to win, and I'm not afraid to work hard.

When I pass through Victory Hall, I notice that the light across from the locker room is on. It's a boardroom we hardly ever use, because we have our best meetings in the locker room. Poking my head in, my eyes sweep the room quickly, already reaching for the light switch to shut it off when I startle. "Excuse me, Coach." I take a step back, while I also bob my head toward our team owner, billionaire Bill Baker, who is sitting across from Coach. "I didn't mean to interrupt." I flash my palms up while I continue to back out.

"Not interrupting." Coach stands up, sliding his chair back at the same time. "You're the person we've been wanting to see."

"Me?" I ask, jerking my thumb to my chest, not recalling any appointments, especially ones while the whole world sleeps.

"Yes." Coach waves me into the room. "Please, come in and shut the door."

Why do I feel like I'm entering a bad scene in a horror movie?

Flashing a look over my shoulder, I swallow and grab the door-knob, pulling it behind me until the normally unnoticeable click echoes, filling the whole room.

"Have a seat." Coach motions to the twelve remaining unfilled seats at the table as he plops back down into his own seat. Suddenly this meeting makes so much sense.

I'm getting fired.

That's one of the caveats to the AHL. They can move guys up or down, or in and out at any time. This is about my backtalking to the ref last night after I had been told I was on my final warning.

I'm clearly on my way out.

I step toward a chair and lower myself down in the pulsating silence all while rolling my hands into tight fists under the table.

I can't believe I blew it.

Coach rubs the stubble on his usually clean-shaven face as he looks above my head, focusing on something behind me. "This is hard for me to say." Then he lowers his gaze directly on me, hooking his light-blue eyes right on mine. "You're not very likable."

My gaze shifts side to side, as I absorb that like a bullet and wait for the part where I'm fired. It's fine if I'm fired but I don't need to sit here and be insulted for ten minutes first. *Just say it!* "I don't care about being liked. I care about winning."

"To clarify, all the guys on the team have your back and say you're an amazing team player, but your public image is trash, and we aren't filling seats."

A lump balloons in my throat. Swallowing, I smooth it for a mere moment before it returns. Forcing air around the lump, I reply, "I know I messed up, but I promise I'm working on it."

Bill speaks up for the first time, leaning in with his eyes firing a light as if he's got the most exciting idea ever. "We're going to help you become popular."

"You are?" I flatten my fists and wipe my sweating palms on my warmup pants.

"We can't stand to lose you. You're an amazing center, and you have the potential to take this team to the top. So, we need to figure out how to help you stick around, and we've devised a plan to do just that. But you must trust us completely."

"I'm not offering you my first-born child, if that's what you're thinking," I joke, trying to lighten the mood, but the sarcasm is lost as their brows furrow in confusion.

"Picture this." Bill flashes jazz hands up in the air, and his eyes light up even more. "Center Axl Erikson is dating celebrity actress . . . who we haven't named yet—"

"I don't date." He's gone too far. I'll do just about anything for this team, but dating to get publicity is not one of them. I don't have time for dating. It's pointless. I have no use for it. Women are evil. That's been my mantra since senior year of high school when my first girlfriend, Susie Marie Jenson, ripped my heart out and stomped all over it by cheating on me with some nerd. We'd dated for most of high school, and I was convinced we'd always be together. I just couldn't fathom how I missed something so huge as her having another boyfriend. I squeeze my fist tightly. Nope. Been there. Not going to date again. I'll stick to hockey.

"You aren't actually going to date," Coach cuts back in. "We'll find some actress to play the part of your girlfriend, and you'll pose for some photos. Fans will show up here just to get a glimpse of her, and we'll leak a few stories to the press, all to get you in a better light—"

"Absolutely not." I roll my eyes in disgust. "I'll work harder, and I'll do your stupid modeling photo shoots for charity, but I'm not going to play some charade."

"What's the big deal?" Coach shrugs his shoulders, holding them up in pause, as if daring me. "It'll only be business. You won't have to like her or hang out with her. Just a few appearances."

"I don't date," I growl, resisting the flashback to how pathetic I had been after Susie broke up with me. I don't ever want to be that vulnerable again.

"Well, good." Coach rises from his chair again, a mischievous smile centering on his face. "Then we won't have to worry about you cheating on your new fake girlfriend."

"I won't cheat on anyone, because there is no one to cheat on." I stand, glad I'm six inches taller than Coach.

"This wasn't an ask. I'm sorry if you are confused, but this is the plan if you want to remain on the team. We have to pay the bills somehow."

"That is dumb." Before I run my mouth more, doing the exact thing I told him I wouldn't do, I close my mouth and gather all my saliva to the back of my throat, swallowing hard. Not talking back is hard.

"Your honesty is what got you in this mess. I'd be careful if I were you." Chuckling, Coach meanders to the door, opening it while standing back to show me my way out. He thinks this meeting is over, but he's delusional.

"Who am I dating?" I blurt out, but then correct my words. "I mean, who is this woman?"

"We're making some calls today and hope to have someone hired by Friday." Bill rises to his feet; his smile is so large you'd think he was practicing for clown college, and he pats me on the back. "This is going to be great."

I suck back a whole lungful of air and dig my teeth into my bottom lip, resisting the urge to form a rebuttal. They haven't even found anyone to play along with this dumb idea, and they won't. Not by Friday. Not ever. They'll get frustrated and give up. I'll pretend to go along with their dumb idea until it fails miserably, and then they'll realize how absurd this is and leave me alone.

Four

SOPHIE

Blowing my rubbed-raw nose, I soak through another tissue and toss it at the white wicker waste basket I conveniently slid next to my childhood bed. In the bustle of my life imploding last night, I ended up confronting Rocco, and some nosy neighbor got it all on video—every tearful moment of him breaking up with me. Within moments the video of me went viral. All my biggest nightmares had come true. I did something reckless and canceled my last two concerts. I hate to disappoint my fans, but there's no way I can perform right now. I don't even want to think about the ticket refunds, or the backlash. I'm really hoping my manager can pull that around for me.

I just can't do life right now.

After committing that potential career suicide, I pleaded for my pilot to fly me to my parent's house in Mapleton, Vermont. I needed to go home to my mom.

My mom is so special because she's more than a mom.

She's always Mama, my best friend, and the only person in the world who will listen and not judge. I don't have to act for her. Even if I tried, she'd see right through it.

With all the paparazzi trying to cash in on this viral story, I can't go out in public, and Mapleton is the only place I feel safe. Everyone here saw me in diapers, and they don't care about my fame. In fact, they are more impressed with that kid from my graduating class who became a meteorologist and now works full-time for The Weather Channel. They talk about him like his ability to predict the weather is a superpower. Yes, his name is Regis, but not *that* Regis. In Mapleton, there is only one Regis, and it's our homegrown weather guy.

I rub my palms into my eyes, wringing out the tears. I can't keep crying this hard. I'm seriously going to get dehydrated. At what point do the tears end?

How did I miss something like this?

My phone vibrates for the hundredth time. Everyone's calling, requesting a statement from me about Rocco's cheating. Live-action breakup gone viral—I wouldn't recommend it to anyone. Crowds gathered, making a clean getaway impossible, and the rest is documented on every social media platform, and even translated into seven languages.

I'm no stranger to public humiliation, and that's not what is upsetting me the most.

It's my heartbreak.

I seriously thought I'd marry Rocco. We had one of those whirl-wind romances that started fast, and overnight we both *knew* we were meant for each other. I rub the back of my neck, desperate to release some of the pressure in my head.

Maybe we both didn't know?

Clearly one of us was confused.

I am jolted out of my thoughts by the sounds of someone knocking on the front door. Rapping echoes from down the hall, and I hold my breath while I wait for one of my parents or my brother to grab the door. I'm not expecting company, but small towns can be odd with neighbors stopping over uninvited. Usually it's Norma, the lady across the street, wanting to drop off some baked goods or tell us about which neighbor we need to pray for this week.

The rapping grows urgent and louder.

I tip my head to hear better, but I don't catch any footsteps going down the hall.

Where is everyone? If they think I'm going to answer that, they are out of their minds. I'm grieving.

Whoever it is, they aren't giving up, and their knocking is almost becoming frantic. What if it's an emergency or something? I want to scream for them to go away, but I'm worried that will feed the Mapleton gossip mill. If I'm unneighborly, my mama will surely hear about it, and she won't tolerate disrespect. "Coming!" I huff while wiping my tears with the back of my flannel sleeve.

I use my shoulder to give my bedroom door more than a gentle shove to open it, as this old house settles in a not-as-functional way, especially in the cooler months. Then I rush down the hall, sliding on the wood floors.

"Coming!" I hiss out right as I grab the doorknob and whip the squeaky front door wide open.

Not Norma.

Two middle-aged men stand on my porch, dressed in athletic warmup pants and Granite Ice sweatshirts—whatever that is. If it's a new church, I'm already sure I don't want anything to do with it. "Hi." I toss a palm out to wave. "No, thanks. I'm a Christian and have a church already."

"May we please have one moment of your time?" The balder of the two gentlemen inserts his heavy black boot on the threshold, tucking it tightly against the door. That's aggressive, and my gaze squirts to the side as I wonder if I need to alert the authorities. I never bring security to Mapleton, but maybe I need to start.

"Depends." I tip my head, hoping this doesn't take all day. "What are you selling?"

"Not a thing," the other man says—this one has lots of hair and teal eyes—and he holds his hands up as if he's under arrest. "We are here to help you get revenge."

"Revenge?" My brows buckle down. "For what?"

"You're Sophie Summers, right?" Baldy cuts in.

"Depends. How did you know I was here?" Suddenly I really want to slam the door. It hadn't dawned on me before I whipped it open in welcome that it could be anyone but Norma. Note to self: check the peep hole before you open the door. Looks like small towns aren't even safe anymore.

"We saw your private plane fly in last night over our arena," Baldy says, as if that is supposed to be a comfort. "Our arena is south of town along Airport Avenue. Your situation is all over the news, and we're awfully sorry, but here's the deal. Your scum fiancé cheated on you, and—"

"Rocco wasn't my fiancé." I practically gasp. At least I hadn't been sold that fake fantasy. I can't imagine how hard this would be if I had been planning a wedding. My throat dries, and I cover my mouth with my palm, so grateful I got away from Rocco before this heartbreak could be any worse.

"Sure," he quips and keeps going. "But we saw you get horribly embarrassed in front of the whole world, and we can help you get revenge."

"The whole w-world," I stutter. This guy is doing nothing to make me feel better about my situation. "I'm not trying to get revenge." Feeling uncomfortable with where this is going, I try to push the door closed, but the door bounces right off the dude's boot. Apparently, he planned ahead for sounding insane.

Are these two hitmen?

Is this how these things go down?

I scan the sky. Partially sunny but hinting of snow later in the day.

Not a good day for murder-for-hire.

Nor would any day be!

I swipe my brow, pulling my mind back to focus.

What am I thinking about here?

These guys are insane and need to leave before they drag me into their insanity, because I'm obviously not thinking clearly. "I'm sorry but I'm not interested in any *revenge.*" I raise my index finger, tracing backwards as if to physically point to an earlier spot on the timeline. "Remember earlier, I led with I'm a Christian."

"Just give us two more minutes, and then we'll leave you alone."

"We will?" Blue Eyes locks the other guy in an eye trap. "Two minutes isn't very much, is it?"

"It's an expression." Baldy dismissively waves his hand. "I'm the owner of Granite Ice, a brand-new and up-and-coming AHL team based right here in Mapleton, Vermont. Our issue is that we need more fans. Ticket sales haven't been the best, and we have this one player who's a pain in the—"

"He's a great catch," Blue Eyes cuts in, as he scratches an itch on his cheek. "He's such a gentleman, and we're hoping we could talk to you about an *arrangement* where you could *work* directly with him for some PR opportunities."

"PR?" I echo. "You want me to sing in a commercial or something?"

"It's more like acting," Blue Eyes clarifies.

"I can act a little, but you'll have to talk to my agent." I toss a look down both sides of the street, thinking how odd it is to have these two guys show up, expecting to hire me like this. Everybody knows you have to go through management. "Her name is Bailey, and she's great. I'll give you her number."

"No agent," Baldy commands, his voice getting deeper. "This needs to be off-the-record."

"You know . . ." Goosebumps spiral up my spine, and I'm getting the total heebie-jeebies. "I'm fine. I'm not currently looking for any work." I shove on the door again, but it won't budge because that guy's mammoth foot is still wedged in the door. "Do you mind?" Losing patience, I point to it, motioning for him to move it. "I listened to your pitch, and I'm not interested."

"Maybe you need to see a photo?" Blue Eyes blurts out, frantically scrolling his phone. "Trust me, I've had my heart broken plenty of times, and the best way to move on is to get revenge. All you have to do is show up to a home game, pose with our star center, and accidentally let it slip that you're dating—"

"What?" I snap, this conversation getting worse by the minute. "You want me to lie about dating someone? Why on earth would I do that?"

"Revenge, remember?" Baldy inserts his stubby index finger in the air between us. "On your cheating ex-fiancé."

"Not my *fiancé*." That word literally digs at my soul. The hurt and pain stabs at my heart, over and over, ensuring I'll never heal from this trust betrayal. At this point, I wish these two were actually pastors of a new church. Sign me up to host coffee and rolls committee even! I can make a mean Jell-o salad for a potluck. *Anything is better than hearing them call Rocco my fiancé.*

"Right, but don't you think it would be nice to see Rocco's smug, arrogant, and haughty face when he sees you snuggled up next to our star center?" Coach slides his phone in front of me. A photo of a super tall man wearing a blue and orange jersey flashes in front of my face. His crew-cut hair is dark and wavy at the tips, which is enough to send my eye sliding down his square jaw, and an electric zap slaps my heart as soon as I land on his pouty lips. My eyes pace his bottom lip back and forth like they are stuck on the bottom loop of a roller coaster. I've never seen a pair of lips that luscious before, and I struggle to keep my jaw from hanging open.

"Excuse me." I exhale, a flush of warm energy rising through my chest. "You want me to take a photo with this *nice*-looking man?" My tongue gets in the way when I say the word nice, and I screech all the while I'm stuck on *those* lips. These two guys really know how to build an argument. This man in the photo is seriously gorgeous, and I have to admit they are right. I'd love to see Rocco's conceited smile wiped right off his face when he sees that I've rebounded so fast.

"Yeah, we'll work out all the details, but that's the basics." Coach pushes the phone a little closer to my face, and the closeup sends another flush of heat to my cheeks.

"I'll do it." My eyes don't move from the photo. I mean . . . way to sell an argument. "For the sake of revenge," I blubber, "I'll take a photo with your baseball guy."

"Hockey," Baldy interrupts. "We are the sport that plays on ice."

My lips form an O, but I don't make a sound. I try to steal another look at the photo, but Blue Eyes drops it to his side.

Baldy adds, "I'm Bill Baker, by the way. I'm the team owner, and this is our coach, Kurt Carlson. We know we have the right guys to win, but winning doesn't always make you money. We need help getting some fans because they are the ones who buy tickets."

I wasn't arguing as I was still a little confused about how they even devised this plan. "I'm not sure how long I'm going to be in town." I pause and wait as an old dually truck races down the road, letting all the neighbors know he's tough, and the scent of diesel gas wafts through the air, irritating my nose. It gives me just enough time to think about this offer, and a shiver runs down my spine. I scan the skyline and think of the oncoming snow. *That must be the reason for my tingles.* As the engine noise declines, I set my eyes back on the coach. "When do you need me to work?"

"How about tomorrow?" Bill suggests. "You can come by the arena after morning practice."

I nod. "I'll be there, and say—" I hold up a finger, pausing. "Can you forward me that picture?" The coach's eyebrow hikes north, and I tack on, "I want to make sure I can remember what he looks like. You know, to make my acting believable." Coach's smile slowly spreads on his face, as if he knows he's struck a chord somewhere inside me.

He can't really know that, though.

Because it didn't happen.

I wave as they stroll back down my walkway, and then I can finally close the front door, confusion swirling in my brain about what just happened.

But one thing is pretty clear.

I'm not crying anymore.

And I know another thing.

I really do wish I could see Rocco's arrogant smirk deflate when he sees I've moved on with someone that hot.

And maybe I really do want revenge. Sweet, sweet revenge.

Five

Axl

A long practice session finally wraps up, and the guys all exit the rink, calling out happy hours to meet up at. Me, I stay on the ice for a few more speed laps. I skate backwards around the rink, instinctively knowing where to turn. I could navigate this place with my eyes closed. My legs are lead after lifting weights before practice, but I'm still going to get off the ice, stretch them out, and go for a run after I leave this place. I never stop training.

As I round the rink a second time, Bill Baker presses both of his giant palms against the Plexi glass, his focus on me. We haven't spoken since the odd meeting yesterday. I can't say I forgot about it, though, as that had to be the strangest request I've ever had from an employer. That includes the time I was required to wear a hot dog hat when I worked at Scottie's Diner the summer after freshman year of college.

Plus, it's not how I do things.

I win by working.

I'm not some pretty boy who uses people or even social media to get ahead. I roll my eyes upward at the mere thought of using social media for fake news publicity, but when I return my gaze to the ground, Bill is still staring at me. "What?" I call out, annoyance budding in my chest. "Did you need me for something?"

"Actually," he says, his speech slow and easy, "since you offered, I need you to take a photo with someone." His gaze slides to the tunnel where a woman stands, but not just any woman.

My throat dries as my gaze slides over her luscious silky mane of ebony hair that cascades down her slender frame, and I halt when I hook on her majestic jade eyes. They literally stun me into immobility.

She's breathtaking.

Bill waves me forward, closer to this decadent woman. "Come meet your co-star, Sophie Summers. She's agreed to take a photo with you."

The name sounds awfully familiar, but I can't place it. I'm re-learning every day not to argue with Bill as he signs my paycheck. Against my better judgment, one skate glides in front of the other, and I advance, eyes locked forward until I step off the ice and join them. I'm cautiously silent as I have one eye on this beautiful woman and the other *more-sus* eye on Bill.

"Just one photo." Bill flashes his phone at us already in camera mode.

"Hi." Her voice is soft and sultry, unlike anything I've ever heard. "You're Axl?" She stands near the wall with a ready-for-business posture.

"That's me," I rasp, still stunned with her beauty. "And you're Sophie?"

She triple nods as if she's also trying to talk herself into this disastrous idea. "Reporting for revenge."

"Excuse me?" I tip my ear closer.

"Yeah, I'm only agreeing to do this to make my ex-boyfriend jealous."

"Whatever," I mumble, reminding myself that I have no desire to start dating and that I don't want to know anything about her. I'm ready to get this whole thing over with so I can get on with my day. I shuffle to stand next to her, my arms hanging loosely at my side. We resemble a police lineup as we gaze forward at Bill and wait for him to snap the stupid photo.

"You're going to have to do better than that." Bill waves his index finger in front of us. "Make me believe this."

Giving Sophie a side-eye, I scoot closer and clumsily lift my arm around her back. She reaches behind me, and we settle together, arms stiffly holding each other and both flashing cheesy smiles at the camera. "Got it?" I mumble through my clenched teeth.

"No." Bill wags his head, disappointment etching his voice. "You have to make it swoony."

"What are you talking about?" My brows crisscross. "There's nothing wrong with my balance."

"Not your balance." Bill walks forward, grabbing my shoulders and pulling me to the center of the tunnel. "This photo needs to melt all the women's hearts and make every guy jealous."

He strides back and grabs Sophie, leading her by the hand to me. When they reach me, he tugs on my arm while guiding Sophie to stand with her back against my chest. Then he physically wraps Sophie in my arms as if I'm pretzel dough. A sonic boom vibrates my whole body, and I'm left numb. This is not the innocent photo Bill had insisted it would be. I'm cradling her *against* my body, and sultry fumes of musky amber waft off her, directly up into my nose. *Nobody warned me about that.* It's a smell of longing, and it slaps a sheet of sweat on my forehead.

"That's better." Bill steps backwards, his phone camera positioned in front of his face, and Sophie and I stand frozen in our pretzel pose as he snaps several photos before he lowers his camera.

I let out an explosive sigh of relief. "Glad that's over," I mumble, dropping my arms to my sides, shaking them off, already noticing that Sophie's scent has been branded into my jersey.

Bill commands something else. "Dip her."

"What?" I snap and not because I have a hard time hearing. I heard exactly what he said, but this is absurd. Nobody wants to see a photo like that.

"Just try it." He waves his index finger in the air again, motioning for us to get back into pretzel formation, and I reluctantly hold out my arm for her to lean back. My lips sandwich together with spite as she folds over my arm. I glare at the camera, waiting for this to be over. "Can you lean over her just a little and gaze into her eyes?" He paces to the left a little to get a better angle.

Can I?

Is that really the question you want to ask me?

Because we both know I *can.*

I also can do the splits and a backflip, but that doesn't mean I should.

What he meant to ask me is how much abuse am I willing to take.

I grind my molars together and lean over, all the while shooting daggers out of my eyes at the camera. *Someday I'll play in the NHL.* I chant all my goals over in my head to remind me why I put up with this stuff. *Someday I'll be rich and can show everyone how tough I really am. Someday I won't have to listen to Bill Baker make these ridiculous demands of me.*

Bill walks forward again, putting his hand on my face, and turning it toward Sophie's. "Can you gaze lovingly into her eyes?"

No, I cannot.

I noisily sniff back a giant breath, holding all my inner dialogue back. *Don't run your mouth, Axl.* "Just take the photo!" I growl, but when he doesn't move the camera, I follow his instruction and let my gaze land on Sophie's. Perfectly green emeralds spiral back light at me as if they're holding a secret. Great, now my palms are sweating.

Bill commands, "Lean a little closer and pucker up, like you're about to kiss her."

Someday I'll be rich and play in the NHL and not have to listen to Bill Baker. I bite my lower lip so hard it hurts, but I refuse to run my mouth.

I can do this.

As dumb as it is.

My heart ticks up a notch and I lean closer, but I'm certainly not puckering up!

That's for sure.

Sophie's chin tips back and her lips part, and all the while her eyes spiral back at me, torching a trail between my eyes and my lips as they drift between the two. The heat that was already firing in my palms starts to blaze a trail right up my arm, not stopping until it plops into the center of my heart. This is the most intensive cardio I've done all year. "Take the picture," I growl.

"Just move your faces together a little closer," Bill instructs, and because I physically can't stand to see how ridiculous this pose is, I close my eyes and tip my chin.

"Got it!" Bill exclaims, and I quickly push Sophie back up and take a step a good two feet away from her.

"Good. I'm hitting the showers." I pivot, unable to take part in this ridiculousness anymore. Someday when I'm in the NHL, I can look back at this humiliation as I count my stacks of endorsement cash and laugh, but that day is not today.

Today I feel used.

I'm not a boy toy. I have serious talent. Just wait until I have several NHL championships under my belt, and this whole charade will be nothing more than a bad memory.

Six

Sophie

"Soph!" Mom hollers as she strolls up the country driveway from getting the mail down by the highway mailbox. The front door cracks open, and I both hear her bellowing and feel the crisp October air creep over the wood floors, chilling my toes.

"What do you need, Mama?" I meet her at the door, ready to close out the cold air for good.

"I was out getting the mail, and Norma came over, and boy, she has some interesting news."

"Who's needing prayers this week?" I roll my eyes. Small-town gossip is too much for me. It's still freezing in our old farmhouse despite the door being closed, and I hug my arms across my chest as I follow Mama back to the living room.

"Apparently you." Mama's green eyes, which match mine, widen with interest while the tips of her lips bend into a smirk.

"Have you been getting swept off your feet by some hockey player?"

"What?" My cheeks glow even though I know exactly what she's talking about. I saw the photo earlier, and I have no idea what photo shopping program they used to make it look so real, but Axl was *hot*. Beads of sweat were rolling down his temples as if he was struggling not to consume me. Just thinking about the photo makes me blush, which is good. I want people to blush. Like Rocco. But I never thought for a second my mama would see it. I drop the weight off one of my legs and lean on the arm of the sofa. "It was a PR thing."

"I don't know about that." Mama pulls out her phone, attempting to scroll for the photo. "It didn't say you were selling anything."

"Not for sales." I cover her phone screen with my hand and stare at her until she locks her gaze back on me. "Just to try to get the team more fans. It's really nothing."

"If you say so." Letting out a suggestive whistle, her eyes widen as she mumbles, "You two do make a lovely couple."

"Mama." I enforce discipline in my tone and slide farther down onto the sofa, twisting my body until I crash flat on my back in the center and cover my face with my hands as I try not to get defensive. "It's just work."

"How do I apply for that job?" Laughter bubbles in her throat, and I give in. We've always been close, sharing our secrets like sisters. I can tell she's not saying many of the things she wants to say, and I appreciate her giving me some space. In a way, it's also fun to hear her tease me about him because he is sooo handsome.

My face heats when I recall how it felt to be in his arms. If he was my boyfriend for real, I'd feel so safe. A special compartment in my heart swells as I think about what it would be like if those photos had been real. Still, it doesn't pay to talk about it because there wasn't much to talk about. Just one photo.

My stomach rumbles for the first time since I got dumped. It's a good sign, as it shows that my appetite is coming back. Before I can ask what's for dinner, my phone vibrates in the center pocket of my oversized sweatshirt, stealing my attention. Bill Baker's name is flashing on the screen.

"I better take this upstairs." I jump to my feet and don't look back, because I can already see my mom's smirk. As I head upstairs, I press the phone to my ear. "Hello?"

"Well done!" he exclaims, a jolly laugh rolling out.

"Thanks." I hesitate, unsure why he's calling when our agreement is finished. "Did you need my agent's number?"

"Nope. I'm calling to invite you to the game tomorrow. I'll get you a box seat right next to me. Best seats in the house. It's the least we can do to show you our appreciation."

"Well . . ." I suck in a deep breath, as hockey isn't my thing, and I search for polite words to say that I want to be left alone. The photo is out, and even my mom is blushing. It's apparently working. "That's awfully nice of you, but I'm afraid I'm busy. I have to reschedule my concerts and get back—"

"Did you happen to see the video of Rocco and that blonde in the Bahamas?"

"What?" My brows bead together as my mind gets whiplash from the sudden change of conversation. "I'm lost."

"Yep, about an hour after we leaked your photo, a semi-blurry image of Rocco and some blonde on the beach in the Bahamas was published on his Instagram."

"Rocco doesn't have Instagram."

"Oh, he does now, and it's filled with photos of him and this lady friend."

This is a game.

I run my hand through my hair and my fingers snag at the ends, reminding me I haven't even brushed it today. It's been one of those recovery days. I don't want to have to do anything, least of all talk about Rocco and some woman. Rocco and I had planned a trip to the Bahamas. I can't believe he took some girl on *our* trip. My heart flips and twists, and now I'm about to throw up. I wish I could be strong and ignore these feelings, but it's still raw. Rocco humiliated me, and even though I vowed to not waste any more feelings on him, I'm disgusted.

Does he think I care who he spends time with?

Does he think I care if he's moved on three days after our public breakup?

He's off on a "honeymoon" with some bimbo, and I'm hiding out in the middle of nowhere, trying to figure out what *I* did wrong. The only thing I did wrong was love him. I wish with all my strength I could flip a switch and get over him, but the amount of anxiety flooding my body right now tells me I'm clearly not.

"You can look it up if you want." Bill's suggestion interrupts my heartbreaking all over again.

"I don't want to see it." Parking one hand on my hip, both to steady myself and assert control, I force myself to accept the situation—and his gift. Clearly God put Bill in my life for this very purpose—to help me cope with this humiliation—and just like that, I'm ready to deal. "What's the plan? Another leaked photo?"

"Come to the game." His voice is smooth, enticing. "Play the role of supportive girlfriend. We'll take care of the rest."

"Okay." I nod, ready to show Rocco I'm not sitting around crying about him. "I'll be there."

Seven

Axl

Some song by the Chainsmokers pulsates through the speakers, and the whole arena jolts into a state of overstimulation as our team skates out for warmups. I circle around our goal, feeling the burn in my hamstrings, before seeing Noah wag his eyebrows toward the owner's box above our goal while letting out a wolf whistle that pricks my ears. "Your girlfriend's here."

What is he talking about, girlfriend? My jaw unhinges, flapping all the way down, and I skate to a halt.

Sophie is standing in the owner's box in front of her seat, daintily waving at me.

That part is relativity *okay.*

The part that makes my jaw stay locked in this wide-open position is the dress she's wearing. Emerald satin loosely hugs her curves, accentuating how trim she is, while doing everything to draw my attention—and the attention of all the warm-blooded men in this room—to her. Green isn't our team color but it's the exact twin to her eyes, and even over the distance between us, I can see her eyes shining back this way—on me.

Who wears a dress to a hockey game? Then again, she's so stunning that she'd stick out even if she was wearing a garbage bag.

All the guys are going to be staring at her.

"Are you going to wave back?" Noah curls a brow as he lowers his stick to the ice and pushes off, leaving me to wonder, *Am I going to wave back*?

This is absurd.

What is she even doing here?

She can't be here to see me.

Does she even like hockey?

We took the photo—a rather sultry photo that's been burned into my brain—and our agreement is done. Bill steps forward from out of the shadow of the owner's box, a full smirk lacing his face as he nods toward me, and I know his game.

But this isn't part of the deal.

Even though warmups just started, sweat beads on my brow. He's drawing this out, but I never agreed to a public appearance. My cheeks fire with anger, and I fight back a scowl as I pivot, lower my stick to the ice, and skate away, not looking back. I will keep my mouth shut. If I can prove I can at least do that, then he doesn't need *Sophie* to show up here to help me be likable.

I keep my eyes to the ice as I join the guys in skating warmup laps and firing off practice shots in the goal. As I skate around, I can't help but notice the arena is more crowded tonight. Almost every seat is full, and people are standing on their feet with their phones posed for photos and positioned as if they're following me.

There are an awful lot more females in the crowd than normal, with entire rows of them in full hair and makeup, looking like they belong on the runway more than a sports arena. Something is up. I skate around to the back of the goal, and several women bat their lashes at me in succession, and then wave with feminine four-finger waves.

I'm over this, whatever it is. The music switches, and I find my gaze floating back up to the owner's box. Sophie's sitting next to Bill, and they're chatting as if they are old friends.

It feels off.

Every man near her is practically drooling over her.

She does look amazing, though.

She catches me looking at her and flashes her palm up in a giant wave. I turn my gaze down, ready to start the game, but even after the faceoff, she remains a flicker in my peripheral vision.

I can't concentrate.

Hockey is always rough, but this game is vicious. I easily score a goal right away, but by the second period, I've gotten slammed against the Plexiglass so many times, that I lose my temper and purposely punch one of their players. That earns them a power play, and I'm banished to the box, but I keep my mouth shut when the ref calls it.

Not losing my temper is a win for me.

Once I'm in the penalty box, my gaze shifts to the owner's box.

There she is with her eyes still locked on me, and as soon as she catches me looking at her, she gestures that soft wave at me again.

Seriously, what's up with that dress?

In a hockey arena, for Pete's sake.

Shaking my head, I turn to watch the game. It takes only a few seconds before my gaze floats back up to Sophie.

What is she doing here?

She couldn't possibly have come here just to watch me.

Bill clearly put her up to this, but our deal is over. So what is he up to now?

Eight

Sophie

I don't know a thing about hockey, but one look at Axl in the rink and I melt.

Still heartbroken, I came here to get revenge on Rocco, but three seconds into this and I've leaped out of heartbreak. I'm ready to tell my mama about *us*.

Book me a chapel and start folding those nappies.

I fan myself, despite the freezing temps. He's wearing his blue and orange jersey, and I never thought about the color orange before, but I'm pretty sure it's my new favorite color. Like a delicious persimmon, sun-ripened to perfection, just waiting for something to pluck him—*I mean it*—off a tree. Drool puddles in the middle of my mouth as I can't stop thinking about persimmons. Yes, that's what I tell myself. The drool is because I'm hungry.

I'm perspiring just watching Axl be so effortlessly hot.

He's a jaguar on skates.

Not to mention those shoulder pads. I fan myself, scanning the arena. No wonder they have the air cranked so much in this place. All the women would be passed out on the floor. All the men look amazing, but Axl's coordination—and how he naturally maneuvers his stick like it's an extension of his hand, keeping the puck perfectly in line as he skates around the rink—explodes my mind. If a genie showed up and offered me one wish, I don't doubt for a second that I'd trade places with that stick.

I don't understand a single thing about the game other than getting the puck in the net, but by the time the game is over, I've entered my *I-love-hockey* era. Not only have I entered it, but I'm also ready to buy all the merch along with season tickets.

"We sold every seat in the house tonight for the first time since we started this team," Bill explains over the crowd cheers. "Tons of your fans showed up to catch a glimpse of you, just like I knew they would." Bill winks at me, adding, "We're onto something."

Tossing a shoulder up in a modest shrug, I avoid any credit. "You seem to have a pretty good team here."

Bill stands, nudges me with his elbow, and quietly leans over. "Why don't you follow me to the tunnel, and we'll snag another photo of the two of you. The fans will go crazy for it."

He's really pushing this fake-dating thing.

The thing is, I don't mind taking photos. It's part of my job, and I've posed with the most random people over the years. Being in front of a camera is easy for me. However, I spent the last two and a half hours drooling over Axl, and I feel like I'm keeping a secret from him now. It's so much different than when I showed up here the other day. Now there are rumors about us. People are watching, interested in our story, and well, I'm sort of intrigued by Axl—to put it mildly.

Bill leads me to the private elevator, allowing us to skip the mass exodus down the steps and the hordes of people. From the elevator, we take a tunnel and end up next to the locker room. A couple of the guys are already dressed in street clothes, carrying their body-sized hockey bags toward the exit. There's a meeting room directly across from the locker room with the light already on, and Bill raises his arm, ushering me to go inside.

I mindlessly enter and my breath hitches in my chest.

Axl's standing in the corner chugging water out of a glass water bottle. He's stripped out of his jersey and wearing a team-colors hoodie with the hood up, partially concealing the side of his face. I easily find the drops of sweat that left a trail from his temple across his flawless cheekbone. The way he devours the water while maintaining a perfect pose makes him look like a model for a bottled water company. I will buy *all* of whatever he is selling.

When he hears the shuffle of us entering the room, he lowers his bottle and turns his gaze on me. For the first time in a long time, I'm nervous about what someone thinks of me. His lips part, but his words are directed at Bill. "Do you mind telling me what you're up to?"

Bill saunters into the room, pulling the door closed behind us, and he doesn't stop until he takes a seat at the head of the empty table. While he joins the pads of his fingers with those on his opposite hand into a perfect contemplation position, he speaks as if the room is filled with people. "I asked you to meet me here because it's working."

From his spot in the corner, Axl flashes a cryptic expression at me, which I return because I'm as lost as he is, and he blurts out, "Do you mind being a little more specific? Why is she here, sitting in your box, and wearing that *dress?*" The word dress comes off as if it's a timebomb, threatening danger to everyone in the room.

Bill chuckles, a hearty series of sounds.

Feeling defensive, I take a step closer to Axl and spew, "I picked the dress."

"Why?" Axl narrows his gaze at me. "Don't you know how to dress for a hockey game? It's fifty degrees in here."

"I didn't." I shake my head back and forth, anxiety bubbling in my gut. Nobody has ever complained about how I looked before. I'm not a diva or anything, but this was Rocco's favorite color on me, and I didn't expect Axl to fawn over me, but I also didn't think he'd be so vocal about not liking the way I looked. "How was I supposed to know that? This is my first time going to a hockey game, and I picked the dress because I wanted to make my ex-boyfriend jealous."

"Jealous of what?" His tone is extra sharp, and he doesn't soften his stony gaze.

"You." A lightning bolt slams through my chest, as I hate admitting how catty I'm being about my breakup. His perfect teeth dig into his bottom lip as if he's lingering on what I said. It's oddly distracting how his lip flushes light pink, then white, and I do everything I can to steal my gaze away from his lips.

His perfect lips.

"You see." Bill cuts in, still flexing his fingers together, "we have an opportunity to help each other out. Axl, I know your goals are to make more money and move up to the NHL. That can't happen if we don't succeed as a team. We need to sell tickets, and you need eyes on you. The NHL wants players who put on a good show, and they aren't going to recruit anyone from a dead team. Did you notice the energy tonight? All the seats were filled. It was magical."

Axl is silent as his Adam's apple bobs up and down. Bill goes on. "And Sophie here, she's in town for the week, healing from her heartbreak. The press was brutal to her about her cheating fiancé—"

"Not my fiancé!" I override him. "He was just a boyfriend, and now he's an ex."

Axl's gaze falls to the ground as a line of contemplation pins between his brows. Silence drags on before he finally lifts his gaze back to me. "I'm sorry you got cheated on. I know how that feels."

Swallowing back the flashback of Rocco and I promising to love each other forever, my jaw quivers. "It hurts."

"You both are dealing with some serious situations," Bill's voice infuses so much enthusiasm you'd think he was leading us to an Olympic medal. "There's no harm in giving the press more positive stories for them to focus on. Then Sophie doesn't have to hear about her ex's infidelity all over." He raises his hand toward Axl, before tacking on, "And you don't have to have the press obsessed with your unlikability. It's a perfect solution for both of you. Plus, we're selling tickets, which means I can offer a bonus. Keep these ticket sales up, and the bonus only grows."

"This is absurd," Axl rasps in disgust. "I'm not lying to people to sell tickets."

Slowly rocking his chair, Bill stares above Axl's head. "Did I ever tell you that when I was in college, I had a roommate for a year. His name was Mike Stevens. You might know the name. He's one of the most successful coaches—"

"In the NHL," Axl cuts, he lowers his voice before continuing. "Are you saying that if I do this, you're going to talk to him about signing me?"

"It's a possibility." Bill nods slowly. "Let's give this thing a good month."

"The NHL has always been the dream." Axl's gaze turns to me, and without pause, he says, "I'm in if you are."

"Whoa, whoa, whoa." I wave my hands in front of me as if someone is coming to crash directly into me. "I'm not sure. All I needed was a photo or two to make Rocco jealous. I also have to get back to work. I can't camp out here in Mapleton for a month. What's in it for me?"

Bill's gaze locks on me, but it's what Axl does that makes my heart motor up. He's clearly all in, already seeing the NHL, and he latches those gorgeous blue eyes on me. "What do you want?"

Triple blinking, I fight the soooo many words that come to my head, words I shouldn't even be thinking. Most of them have to do with his lips on mine. I didn't hate the chance to meet him. I enjoyed watching the game tonight and would look forward to seeing him play again. But I'm in this to make Rocco jealous, and Axl's going to have to play, too. "Rocco went on a vacation with some woman, but we had planned that trip together. We also planned a black-tie charity fundraiser together, and neither one of us can cancel, despite our breakup, because it's this weekend. I'm sure he'll be there with her, or some other bimbo. I want you to come to New York with me so I don't have to face him alone."

"Deal," he confirms too fast, and he throws his hand out in front of me. "Shake on it."

I chuckle as this whole thing seems foolish. Yet, as his calloused palm scratches at my skin, it lights a spark in my arm that assures me his weathering is the best kind. He's strong. Focused. Determined. And I take comfort in that when he gives my palm a confirming squeeze.

"We have to set rules, though." Axl drops my hand, placing both hands on the back of a chair in front of him. "This is professional. We take photos in public together, but nothing ever crosses that line."

"I think we're safe there." I motion toward the exit. "We're at a hockey arena, and I'm watching you play. There's no chance for anything to cross any lines."

"What about in New York? That's obviously different because it's going to look like a date."

Heat burns my cheeks as I think about spending time with Axl, even if it's a fake date.

"I think we only need one rule. No kissing."

He nods. "Right. There will in no way be any kissing. That's an absolute must. Anything else?"

I tip my head, thinking. I have the upper hand in this negotiation. I'm going to move on from Rocco no matter what happens, and frankly, after tonight I mostly have. I don't want to appear too eager to agree to this, and there is something that would be fun to throw out there. "One more thing."

"What's that?" His face becomes alert, eyes pinning on me with laser focus.

"Grow a beard."

His eyes shift from side to side before he smirks awkwardly. "Why? Does your ex not like beards?"

"This isn't about him." I run my tongue over my bottom lip, hydrating it. "I like beards."

His gaze hovers over mine, and for a moment I swear I see a flicker in his eyes, but Bill inserts himself back into the conversation. "Sounds like a plan. And like any good plan, we need to review. Sophie agrees to come to the games and watch Axl, posing for a photo or two. Axl agrees to go to New York for a charity thing, and both of you agree that under no circumstance will there be any kissing."

Without pause, Axl nods. "Agreed."

I hang back against the wall. This is happening sort of fast, and I don't have time to think about any potential downsides.

I guess it can't hurt anything. "Same."

Bill declares, "It's settled."

I bite the inside of my cheek, trying hard not to flush warm, as an announcer calls in my head, "*Let the games begin.*"

Nine

Sophie

I bring Mama's good mixing bowl filled with peeled hard-boiled eggs over to the counter, right next to the six one-quart mason jars all lined up in a row. "Is this a new recipe?" I quirk my brow toward Mama, as she's an avid gardener and a fierce homemaker, but I don't recall her ever canning boiled eggs.

"It's not a recipe as much as it's an invention." A chuckle rolls from her perfectly painted lips. "Norma is the one who started canning eggs. You know all her recipes are bland as sawdust, so I doctored this up." Mama lifts a bowl of julienned jalapeños peppers, then she motions to the chopped garlic and onions, already prepped on the counter. "They turn the eggs a neon green, but they'll clean you all the way out. I haven't gotten so much as a tickle in my throat since I started eating these."

"That's disgusting." I fake a dry heave, but I'm still smiling.

"You say so now, but wait until you try them." Taking a ladle, she starts to scoop out the peeled eggs and drop them one by one into the wide-mouth jars.

When the first jar is full, I reach for it. "I take it I'm supposed to fill this with water."

"Oh, no." She waves me out of the way, grabbing the jar back from me. "It's a warm, spiced vinegar solution."

"Does it get much spicier than jalapeños?"

"I like to let them soak for a least a few days, but you'll be able to test them out for Sunday dinner."

"Oh, about that." I pause and wait for Mama to fill the last jar. Then I come over with the cloves of garlic, dropping a few into each jar. "I'm going to run back to New York for the weekend, but I'll be back on Monday at the latest."

"You're not going after Rocco, are you?" Her eyes nervously pace my face, sadness etched in the downward pull of her lips.

"No, it's not like that at all." I find the side of my cheek and trap it between my teeth for a nice squeeze while I decide on the best words to use. I don't want to lie, but Mama doesn't need to know all the details. "I'm going to that charity dinner Rocco and I organized. I didn't feel like it, but Rocco isn't staying home, and I know he'll be there with some new girl, and the press will be all over that. Axl agreed to come with me, so we're going together."

"I'm so glad you brought up Axl." Mama's lips purse to the side, hinting an opinion is about to come. "What exactly is this all about? You said he was a business partner, but Norma and her reliable church friends are showing me some photos, and I don't ever recall any marketing campaign looking so cozy before—"

"Mama!" I don't even blush, as I'm fighting a fit of giggles. Neither one of us would ever call Norma's gossip friends—*reliable church friends*. "I know the photos are a little *more* than I had originally thought they would be, but the bottom line is that everything is innocent. It really is just a PR move, something to get the focus off Rocco and to help Axl out. You know I wouldn't lie to you. And . . ." I bob my head side to side as I weigh *how* honest I want to be, but I'm dying to tell someone, so I spew it all in out in one big rush. "He's insanely cute, and it's a bit exciting to have his attention. It's keeping my mind off Rocco, and that's helping me heal."

"I see." Mama's lips purse out again, and I wait for her second dose of opinion, but instead she smirks. "Hand me those jalapeños."

The back door squeals open, and heavy boot stomps echo from the mud room before Dad emerges, wearing his hunting camouflage. "Hey, you two good-lookings," he sings out, his lips teasing a smile while he crosses the room to Mama and kisses the top of her head. "What ya got cooking?"

"Canning eggs." Mama moves along the row of jars, filling each one with a healthy dose of jalapenos. "Did you get anything?"

"Nope." Dad shakes his head, regret etching his brow. "Not unless you count two giant blisters on the backs of my heels and a brand-new crick in my knee that wasn't there yesterday."

"That sounds about right." Mama and Dad's laughter blend together, tugging at my heart strings. It's been a while since I spent real time at home. My work is nonstop with constant pressure to have a new song out or to book another concert, not to mention how I was flying all over the country to make Rocco a priority. I'm overdue to spend time here. Maybe this arrangement with Axl is good for a lot of things.

Ten

Axl

"Over here!" Sophie waves from the nearly empty airport parking lot as I pull in right at sunrise. She's wearing cotton candy pink from head to toe, with cuddly-looking sweatpants and a matching hoodie, making her look casual as she waits for me.

Casual and maybe a little snuggly.

I throw my truck into park and grab my backpack, strapping it on my shoulder, and jump out while tossing her a silent wave. The sky is clear, despite the fall season, which is displayed so well on the multicolored trees to the south of the airport. A large commercial plane waits near the building, parked by a ramp, but I head to the little jet out in the center of the parking lot.

I've never flown on a private jet before. I'm most excited about the convenience of not having to go through the main terminal and security, even though Mapleton's airport is tiny with only one gate. It makes me think about my dreams of reaching the NHL and having enough money to do all the things I've always wanted to do, especially traveling. Someday I'll have so much money that I'll have my own plane parked out here, and a whole staff of people willing to wait on me.

"Are you ready for this?" Sophie calls out, breaking my thoughts. Even in the morning without makeup, Sophie looks radiant. The rising sun catches her smile enough to light up her whole face. I must say, if I have to pretend to date someone, it definitely pays to work with someone this gorgeous.

"I am ready, and good morning," I say as our steps sync up, striding forward to the small plane. "Are you ready?"

"I think so." Her brow is serious as she tugs a full-sized rolling suitcase forward.

"Let me get that." I reach out instinctively, latching my hand around the handle. For a moment our hands brush each other's, sending a tingle up my arm. Unprepared to feel shivers, I blink until they simmer, and then I throw on a teasing smile. "This is all for one night?"

"In a sense."

"What do you mean in a sense? It either is or it isn't."

"I came prepared with a dress for tonight, shoes and that whole thing, but I also brought street clothes in case we do anything else, and clothes for tomorrow and snacks."

I wince and bite my lower lip. I'm not sure I can handle another one of her dresses. It's hard to think about anything else when she's dressed up. One thing I never counted on when I agreed to this whole thing was how hard it would be to not feel a magnetic attraction to my fake date. I lower my gaze to the ground and focus on my walking as it's a decent distance to the plane. Of course, I hadn't known before we started who I'd be matched up with, but if I give Coach credit for anything, I'd say he's excellent at hiring people. One of the bonuses to fake-dating someone who lives in a different zip code is when all this is done, we'll more than likely never see each other again, and all this attraction can be left to simmer.

When we reach the bottom of the steps, a man and woman are standing by the open door. Both are wearing blue avian-style clothing and greet us with too-large-for-this-early-in-the-morning smiles. "Morning," Sophie rings out while motioning to me. "This is Axl, and he's flying with us on this trip." She dips her head in the opposite direction, saying, "This is William, my favorite pilot, and Skye, our flight attendant."

"You're a flight attendant, and your name is Skye?" I smile at the lady, who simultaneously reaches forward and takes the handle of Sophie's bag. She has a perfect hair bun pinned on the back of her head and a cherry-red smile.

"I didn't even have to make that one up." Skye motions smooth-ly like every flight attendant does, inviting us into the plane. "Go ahead and get comfortable. I'll be right up, and we can take off as soon as the plane is secured."

Sophie takes several steps ahead of me, ascending the steps, be-fore tossing a look over her shoulder. "You coming?"

"Yeah." I struggle to make my legs move. This whole event is sur-real, and I want to absorb everything. *There's a private jet waiting for me to ride in it.* I can't believe this is how some people live. "Do you always travel like this?" I drag my legs up behind her, slower than my normal pace, looking at everything with care. There are three rows of seats with a wide leather recliner on each side, and it has a brand-new plane smell. Not that I've ever smelled a new plane before, but it couldn't be any other smell.

"I do, and yes, I know how lucky I am. I flew commercial and even rode a bus for a lot of years." She crosses the aisle, plops down into the first recliner, and immediately straps her seatbelt and kicks up the footrest. "You can sit wherever you like."

Taking the recliner opposite hers, I'm more intentional as I feel how nice the leather is and notice the ample room to stretch out. There's even a cup holder ready for a beverage and a large TV screen in front of me. I've never experienced anything like this, and I blink several times, hoping I don't wake up. "We travel all the time," I say, finally breaking my speechlessness, "but this is not the kind of traveling we do. I could get used to this."

"I'm sure if you keep working hard, you'll get one of these someday, too." Her expression is thoughtful, not at all something you'd expect from someone who lives this lifestyle.

"That's the plan." I inhale, taking in the scent again, as everything in this plane feels and looks brand new. "I love playing hockey, and it's definitely my dream job, but I'm ready to see the world."

"You like to travel?" She pivots in her chair, getting a more direct glance at me. "What is your dream place to go?"

"I don't know if I have just one, but I'm more about doing outdoorsy things since I spent my life inside an arena. I want to swim in all the oceans and hike secret trails in foreign countries that only the locals know about until I'm so tired I fall asleep in the middle of the forest in a hammock. Then after I wake up, I'll head back to some renovated castle I've rented for my stay."

Her gaze stares off above my head, and her voice wafts out a little dreamily. "Wow, you have thought about this, haven't you?"

"Haven't you?" I pull my brows up, as I can't stop thinking about what my life will be like when I finally get ahead.

"No." She wags her head back and forth. "I just work, and before last week, I spent all my free time running after Rocco and his intense schedule. I guess I have time for a hobby now that I'm single. All of those things sound amazing, actually." Though her words end optimistically, her gaze lowers to the ground.

My heart twists the same way it did when I first heard about her ex cheating on her. She looks so broken, and as much as I hate this charade, I do feel bad. I know exactly what it feels like. "I'm sorry about what you're going through. If it's worth anything, I've been there, and it gets better."

Lines of contemplation stack on her forehead. "You were cheated on?"

Holding my breath, I pause. I can't believe I'm admitting this, and it seems like another lifetime ago, but in an odd way I'm hoping to cheer her up by offering the hope that life moves on and it's not worth dwelling on the losers who hurt you. "It was in high school by my first girlfriend. She had a side guy for quite a while, but I didn't see it because I was so busy with hockey."

"That stinks." Her breath blows out. "How'd you find out?"

"I was supposed to leave for a weekend hockey tournament, but a forecasted storm ended up shutting down all the highways, and the bus couldn't leave. I was relieved because I hadn't had much time to spend with her, and as soon as I had the word, I rushed over to her house without calling." I glide my hand over the soft leather armrest, feeling silly to find comfort in something so trivial but it helps me to get the words out. "All I wanted to do was surprise her, but instead I caught her with him."

"Ah, that's exactly how I found out!" Her voice ticks up before our gazes connect on a level of comradery. "Did it feel like you died?"

"Nope." I wag my head, fully remembering the very real pain. "It felt like my heart was ripped out, but I was fully alive and living through the pain. It was the worst thing I had ever experienced, which is why . . ." I pause, realizing how I'm sharing all the things I never tell anyone.

"Why what?" She leans closer, nervous anticipation spiraling out of her eyes.

I scratch the back of my head, wishing I had kept my mouth shut. I need to start taking Bill's advice more seriously. "Ah, why . . . I never dated after that."

Her brows spring up. "You haven't had a girlfriend since high school?"

"Nope, and don't plan on having one ever again. I'll stick to hockey."

Before Sophie replies, Skye peeps her head in from behind the curtain. "The captain is ready for takeoff. Is there anything you need before we taxi?"

"I'm good." I shake my head, returning my gaze to my side of the plane, glad for the interruption. I sure wasn't expecting to spill all my secrets first thing in the morning. This whole trip has me acting totally different than my usual self. "No, thank you."

"I'll have a pillow, blanket, and some carbonated water," Sophie rattles off like it's the most normal thing in the world to have people fuss over her. Skye crosses the cabin to the closet while we taxi. I ponder that it sounds normal because this really is Sophie's life, even if it's mind-blowing.

"I hope you don't mind." Sophie retrieves her blanket and pillow from Skye. "I'm going to nap. I haven't been sleeping at all these last few days." She positions the pillow behind her head, tugging it back and forth to shimmy it into the perfect position.

Skye returns behind the curtain, and we take off. I'm left alone with my thoughts, the strongest being, *What a life. I'll do anything to get this life.*

"Axl," Sophie's voice calls me to look back over at her. Her eyes are wide and honest as if I can see directly into her soul. "I'm sorry about that girl. She was a fool for cheating on you." I lower my gaze, ready to give a rebuttal when she beats me to it, "I know this whole thing is a little weird for us both, but I'm glad you're here."

My heart ticks up a notch before I look up. She closes her eyes and rests her head back against her pillow again. Soon, her shoulders are rising and lowering in steady restful breaths. She looks so peaceful and beautiful. I bite the inside of my cheek, forcing down my thoughts from going any further than that. I can admire a beautiful woman, but it has to stop there.

I don't date.

"You've been really quiet." Sophie lowers her phone, staring at me from her spot in the back seat of our car. It's not Uber, or even a cab, but a private car that picked us up right on the tarmac. That part I almost expected. But the part that made me look twice was the driver had Sophie's iced coffee order already in her cup holder. Yes, there is an even cooler part—a bottle of my favorite electrolyte-infused water was in mine. I didn't even know she knew what I drank, but she shrugged her shoulders and said her agent had done some internet snooping on me when she set up everything. I can't believe people live like this.

"I'm sorry. I'm not trying to be quiet." I blink a couple of times. "I'm just absorbing this lifestyle of yours, and it's hard to wrap my brain around it."

"I can see that." She quietly sets her phone next to her, clearing her hands. "If you would have told me even three years ago that this would be my life, I wouldn't have believed you. It's crazy how fast you get used to it and how fast you forget to appreciate it. It took me working my butt off through all of my teens and most of my twenties to get to this point. Prior to this, I spent my time touring radio stations for morning shows, and through all that, I always needed my parents' support and a few waitressing jobs on the side."

Thankful that she was opening up about her private life after everything I spilled out on the plane, I lean closer. "How did it change?"

"What do you mean?" Her brows furrow together. "How did I get my big break?"

"Yeah. For me, I have my eyes on the NHL because that means better pay, better endorsements, better interviews, etc. I'm sorry, I don't follow pop music, so I'm not really versed on your career. Was it like one song that changed everything?"

"I wish." A sarcastic chuckle blurts from her lips. "I got up, did the grind, and made a little bit of progress each day. Maybe I made one new fan at the radio station I was at that day, or I was able to share my music with someone I waited on at my night job. It slowly accumulated. After I had a decent number of fans, I was able to get a better production company and a better PR company. That took all my profits and more, but it kept the momentum going. When I started dating Rocco, things fell into place because I started getting free PR just by being next to him, but again, that had a downside, too. Once they are in your private life, they never leave." She turns her head toward the window, her brows rising. "Here's the hotel. My manager booked us rooms at the same place the dinner is at."

My mind replays her words. She just admitted her career took off from being with Rocco, which is the exact same thing the coach set up for me. Maybe Coach is right, and this will help me to launch my career. Now that I think about it, talent might not be enough anymore. It seems like everyone needs a platform of some sort as well, and this could be the break I've been waiting for.

"Yeah," she says, stealing my attention back. "We won't have to hurry to leave, and we'll have plenty of time to relax. My manager usually books me some time at the spa if it's open, and I requested one for you, too."

"Nice life." I sigh and set my jaw while I gaze out the window, anticipation fluttering through my gut at all the lifestyle upgrades I'm getting this weekend just by being with Sophie. It's a whole other class of treatment.

Someday.

But maybe if Coach is right, that someday will come sooner than I thought.

I haven't worked this hard for all these years to quit now, and I'm closer to my dreams every day. If acting like I'm dating Sophie makes me more likable, and if it helps the team, I'm going to give it my best performance and treat it like it's my one shot.

Eleven

Sophie

"Are you checking into your suite, Miss Summers?" the concierge calls out as soon as Axl and I cross the threshold in the vast hotel lobby. I home in on the unusual amount of people milling around the entrance area. They part to the sides, clearing a path for us, while many take out their phones for obvious reasons and whispers buzz through the whole room.

"Yes." I stride to the desk as Axl guides my suitcase, and onlookers aren't shy about taking photos.

"I have two adjoining suites for your comfort," the concierge declares, and the crowd hushes as everyone appears to be eavesdropping. "And just to confirm, your couple's massage is in one hour in the spa."

"Couple's massage?" I echo, jolting my head back before catching myself. The slew of people are still hanging onto every word of this conversation. "That sounds . . . *great*." I can't even look at Axl, because if he gives me any sort of confused look, I won't be able to keep this fake grin on my face. The thing is, my manager, Bailey, booked my massage, and I made the point to tell her to add Axl but only as a friendly gesture. I didn't think for a moment she'd book a couple's massage. To ensure this weekend is a success, I haven't told anyone but my mom that it isn't a real romantic getaway, and now I'm dealing with some of those repercussions.

Bailey thinks Axl and I are dating, and she set up our accommodations for a couple.

We take our keys and pivot together, while I make sure to walk as closely as possible to him, hoping to give off the illusion that we're together. We're all toothy smiles the entire way, even when we get upstairs to our hallway. I don't trust that someone isn't hiding in the shadows, ready to pop out to catch us out of character. I hold my breath as Axl swipes the room key, and we both enter the same room. As soon as the door clanks behind us, I let out a defeated sigh. "That was so much harder than I thought it would be. Did you see all the people staring at us?"

"I think Bill tipped off social media to where we are staying for a little extra PR, but I didn't think it would be like that. Your fanfare is unreal." He beams back at me, but I know the smile isn't about me. He's been starry eyed this whole trip as he lives my life with my private plane and crew of people who fawn over me.

"Trust me, this is unusual for me, too. Did you notice that most of the people taking photos were women? And they were clearly zoomed in on you with your week-old beard." I smile, hoping he receives that as a compliment. His brows pin together in a serious manner, but he's quiet. Hopefully, I didn't offend him, and I rush to change the subject, "Hey, I do want to say, I'm sorry about the couple's massage. I had my manager book it, but I totally forgot that she doesn't know this is fake dating. I had no idea she'd do that. You can go, and I'll stay here."

"No, it's not a big deal. You were more excited about it, and you should go." He parks my suitcase against the wall and crosses the room to the adjoining suite door. Without even scanning the massive suite, he unlocks the door and walks through it, calling back, "You can have the main suite. I'll stay here."

I hadn't for a second thought we'd share a room, but he looked almost uncomfortable even standing in my room. It was almost as if he couldn't get away fast enough. He's not upset about the couple's massage, is he?

That was not my doing.

I would never put either one of us in that situation.

It would never happen either, because one of us can just skip it or even both of us.

It's crazy to think we'd do something like that.

We barely know each other.

True to his word, Axl stays locked up in his room while I sneak down to have my massage, and it is a true "sneaking" situation. I case along the wall of the back staircase, and I still find several fans loitering with their phones handy. It's worth it, though, because my massage is amazing, releasing so much shoulder tension that my whole body melts like a pad of butter.

When I sneak back upstairs to change into my gown, the hairstylist I use when I'm in New York is already waiting for me. Everything goes well, and before I know it, it's time for us to head downstairs. For the first time since Axl disappeared into his room, he taps on the adjoining door.

"Come in," I call out while I stare in the mirror and press my new lip liner to the top of my lip, trying to cheat my lip line. I love the natural makeup look my stylist gave me, but one thing I'm big on is full lips.

I hear the door push open and close, but I focus on the mirror as I diligently fill in the gap, careful not to smudge it. When it's perfect and just the way I like it, I snap the cap back on my liner and casually pivot.

My breath hitches intensely, inflating my chest.

Axl's wearing a cobalt suit, with the blue setting off his eyes, and the tailoring on his suit adds so much swagger.

And the freshly sprouted beard. Oh, Martha. He wears it so well.

I manage to keep my mouth closed. Resisting the urge to drool, I swallow it down.

Then swallow again for preventive measures.

And once more.

Why did I just pencil on my lips with so much detail?

"You look . . ." He lets out a sigh that borders a groan, and I'm not sure if that's a happy sound or not. His gaze takes a sweep over me, before latching on to my eyes, and I swear it left a scorching trail on my skin. "Radiant," he tacks on, all the hues of blue in his eyes spiraling back at me.

This moment doesn't feel like a fake date.

This moment feels real.

Again, I have to swallow to protect my fake lip line at all costs. I smile with pinched lips, keeping the flood-gates closed, hoping it passes for a mysterious smirk instead of the more likely constipated smile.

"Are you ready for this?" he asks when I don't reply to his compliment. I literally can't speak. My throat feels like it's been baked into hardened clay. The way he's looking at me, and the way he's *looking* in that suit, make speaking an impossibility.

The beard was a *good* call.

I do the next best thing to talking. I hum out a giant, "Mm-mum." Then I hook my arm in his, and we head out.

Twelve

Axl

"My ex is right over there in the corner," Sophie whispers under her breath as we do our best to glide into the room, chins up and arms entwined. I swallow as I scan the large banquet room, which is eloquently decorated in fall crimson and gold. A small band is set up in the corner, playing light jazz. Everyone's dressed in cocktail coats and dresses, taking petite steps as they meander through the crowd, flashing their freshly whitened smiles. My stomach flips at the strong aroma of clashing perfumes and colognes, and I long for fresh air. "If you think it looks like he's in the NFL," Sophie continues, "it's because he is. He also has a terrible temper, and he doesn't get along with most people because he's very violent."

Of course, I knew she had dated Rocco Bella, an NFL superstar, but I didn't need the ab-lib about his temper or what a bully he is.

Just like she says, he's off in the corner. Dressed for the occasion in a black suit. He has beady eyes and an oversized nose that looks like it's been broken more than once. He's surrounded by several people, including a female on his arm, but his gaze lasers on us. I can't give him the satisfaction of seeing me return his inquiring stare. Even though I've never met the guy, cheaters are all the same, and I'll go on record to say I hate them all. "I really don't care to talk about that jerk."

I guide her farther into the room and with each step we take, I can feel another set of eyes latch onto us. I know I'm here to perform, and I'm used to people watching me, but not like this. Usually, I'm focused on getting a puck and don't have time to notice who is nudging who as I pass. This is slow motion, a torture I've never experienced. Of course, it is quite ego-inflating to have Sophie on my arm. She is so radiant, she practically glows, and people just naturally gravitate toward her. It makes me consider how stupid Rocco must be—a few too many blows to the head or something—because no other woman in the room even comes close to being as gorgeous as Sophie.

Not that I'm looking.

It's just a fact.

"Should we get something to eat?" Sophie motions to the rows of tables draped in white linen cloths and layered with so much decadent food that you'd think this was a presidential reunion. It was an outright buffet with everything from ribeye and lobster on one end, to cheesecakes and tiramisus on the other.

"If you want something, I'm happy to walk over there, but it's a little early for me." I don't tell her that my stomach is a pit of nerves. Over the last few hours, I've somehow become personally invested in the outcome of this event. I could care less about these high-society dinners, but thinking of Rocco cheating on Sophie brought me back to a place I swore I'd never return to. Ever since this morning when I opened up to her about my ex, the memories of feeling as if my heart was being ripped out of my chest had come flooding back in nearly overwhelming ways. And the hard part is, when I went through my healing journey, I did it privately on the ice, but poor Sophie had everything aired out in the public eye. I can't imagine how she can be in the same room with him and holding her head so high. She sure is strong, and it makes me so proud of her.

My gaze snakes its way over to the corner. It's clear by the way Rocco has a woman practically crawling up his sleeve that he's doing it intentionally to make Sophie jealous. My bottom lip rolls in as I attempt not to look in his direction. *I can't stand a cheater.* "Maybe later then." She pivots, scanning the room, and motions to the other side. "Should we check out the silent auction?"

"That sounds wonderful." I'm eager to have something to focus on to avoid the people gawking at us, and we cut clear across the room to the tables in the back. I point to the homemade baskets of goodies. "It's not a silent auction without the desserts."

"Right?" She laughs airily, and we both slowly pace along the rows. "I'd like to find something to bid on to help out, but I can't do all the calories."

"It looks like they have art further down, and I see some pottery and things . . ." My voice drops off as I pick up a picture frame with Sophie's photo. "Look at this. It's a framed list of a prize package that includes a photo and lunch with you. Did you know about this?"

She waves her hand dismissively. "I do that every year as my donation. My manager always submits it, so I haven't even thought about it." She leans over on one foot, reading the bidding log. "What in the world?" Her words fog together while her feathered brow hikes. "What does Rocco think he's doing?" She jabs her perfectly manicured finger on the paper. "Rocco bid on it. That can't happen. I'll file a restraining order before I let him win this."

"Is that a joke?" I narrow my gaze, hyper-focusing on the names, and sure enough, the name on the bottom is Rocco Bella with a bid for a thousand dollars. I grab the pen and scribble my name below his, upping the bid to two thousand. I don't have an extra two grand lying around as I'm still paying off my stupid student loans, but there's no way I'm letting that creep win a date with Sophie. Not after what he did to her.

"You don't have to do that." She grabs my arm, gently guiding me away from the table. "I didn't mean to make a big deal about that. I'm sure someone else would have outbid him."

"He's a creep to even put you in that situation after what he did to you." I grind my back molars and glare at him. This time I don't mind one bit if he catches me looking at him. He should just bring it.

Sophie must feel the tension shifting, because she tries to bring my focus back to the auction. "Oh, look, a Tiffany necklace." She scoots in front of the silver chain. "I can bid on—" Her voice drops off and I already know why.

Rocco strides right up to her photo-and-a-date item and proceeds to upbid me. Blood bubbles in my veins, starting at the tips of my fingers, and I flex my fingers out before rolling them into a fist. The bubbles continue up my arm, pumping adrenaline into my chest, and anger ignites. I draw in a deep slow breath. Sophie must sense it because she places a cautionary hand on my arm. "He's not worth it."

"There's no way he should even be allowed to talk to you, let alone bid on that."

"I'm sure he doesn't actually want to go. It's more just his way to show who's boss. He's rich and can show off by outbidding you and everyone else. Please, don't add another bid. I can find a way to have him disqualified."

"I'll disqualify him right here." My fists tighten, while my nostrils flare. He may be in the NFL, but he's about to meet his worst nightmare. Sophie may not be my girlfriend, but she is my date. I brought her here tonight, and as long as she's with me, I will protect her.

"Excuse me, sir." A lady, wearing a white tuxedo shirt and black slacks slides in front of Rocco. "This auction doesn't allow for dual bids. You get one chance to vote, and if someone upbids you, you're done. I'm sorry, but you'll have to move on to other items."

Blinking hard to avoid laughing, I turn to Sophie, and she too is rolling her lips in. "Let's get out of here," she whispers, pulling me far away from the auction tables. "That was too close for me. You almost put a fist through his face."

I wasn't laughing anymore.

She's right.

I didn't lose my temper, but I was fully ready to disqualify him in my way. With all the cameras already on us tonight, that is not the kind of PR either of us need. My anger is still running high, I'm not going to let Rocco ruin our night. I jerk a thumb over my shoulder back to the food. "Don't you want something to eat before we leave?"

"You know . . ." Her shoulders rise and fall, bringing her eyelids down a notch, too. "I'm more tired than I thought I would be. This week has been draining." She tosses a glance over her shoulder back to the food tables and the still-growing crowd of people. "We made our public appearance, and I want to leave."

"Are you sure?" I give her the once over, seeing how her updo is still perfectly in place, and her dress—man, can this girl wear a dress—is ready for a full night out. She must have spent hours getting ready. I don't want to be the reason she goes home early. "I promise not to punch anyone."

"I think we can quit while we are ahead."

"I'm sorry if you think I screwed this up." I lower my tone, and we both start to pace toward the exit. "If you want me to leave, and you can stay, I will. We just walked in the door. I hate for you to miss the event *you* coordinated."

"It's fine." Her eyes seem weary when they wash over my face, but I don't buy that as the sole reason she's ready to leave. We didn't even eat dinner.

She's disappointed in me.

We didn't even make it fifteen minutes, and I was about to lose control of my actions. Coach is right about my temper. Maybe this is something I do need to work on. Being raised in a hockey rink, aggression was encouraged. I don't remember when I started to let it blend into the rest of my life, but it needs to stop. I trail behind her several long steps as my shame hangs heavy in my chest. We make it back to our suites, and she enters first, not looking back at me, before I step forward to follow, but something catches my eye.

A paparazzi is standing with his phone camera posed, and it appears he got something on camera. Probably us not acting like a couple, as I wasn't even walking next to Sophie. "Hey," I growl. "Who do you work for?"

"Celebrity Sightings," he quips, tucking his phone into his coat pocket while he takes long strides backwards. Clearly, this isn't his first rodeo, and he's prepared to flee to keep his footage.

"Can you delete my photo, please?" My breath quakes on the inhale, and everything I just told myself about keeping my temper goes out the window. I'm about to mess this whole thing up for Sophie, but I have a chance to save *it* if I get him to delete that image.

"Have a nice night, sir." He waves while spinning on his heel and bolts out of the hallway.

I could run after him.

I could beat him to the ground and steal his camera.

My legs twitch under my weight as they wait for my command to chase him. But I remember the disappointment on Sophie's face when I almost lost my temper just a few moments earlier. Even if I got the photos back, I might cause a bigger scene for her by beating him up.

That isn't worth it.

I stand back, wringing my hands together.

It seems like no matter what I do tonight, I'm going to disappoint Sophie. Guilt creeps into my gut. I hadn't realized I put so much pressure on myself before now. Sure, I had selfish reasons to agree to do this, and it was all about me making it to the NHL, but now that I'm here, I want her to have a victory, too. I blew it.

Thirteen

Sophie

The next morning, I'm up before the sun rises, ready to fly back to Mapleton. I didn't need to leave because of my schedule, but I've learned it's better to avoid public crowds. I sip the coffee I made in the little coffee maker, but it's weak and tasteless, and I can't wait for the strong stuff from the coffee shop that my driver always has ready for me. As I make a final sweep of the hotel room, checking for forgotten items in the bathroom, I can't help but feel heavy this morning.

I'm not depressed, but I don't have the satisfactory glow I assumed I'd have from showing up at that event with a handsome date. It doesn't even have anything to do with Rocco's bidding on my date. That's just Rocco being Rocco. I more or less feel like I'm already over the drama. Maybe the press never will be, but I know my truth. I don't need to put on a show for Rocco or anyone else—other than my concerts of course, but I get paid to do that. I'm ready to put this stupid fake-dating thing behind me. I'm already adding it to my list of been there, done that, and things I'll never do again.

My phone vibrates right as I drop my makeup bag into my suitcase. I don't even need to confirm who it is, because Bailey is always on top of things. I push the button to send the call to the speaker phone as it's way too early for FaceTime. "Morning, Bails," I ring out. I'm the only one of us who thinks the play on *Frere Jacques* is funny, but I do it every morning.

"Morning, Sophs. Making sure you don't oversleep."

"No, wide awake and almost out the door." I plop down on the edge of my bed, taking a moment to rest.

"You didn't happen to see the latest news about your love affair, did you?"

"Now what?" I smile each time I hear that I'm in a love affair. If only people knew that we hardly knew each other.

"I guess some guy got photos of you going into your room last night, and you were walking like half a hallway ahead of him and didn't even look at him. It looks very stiff. He's calling your whole relationship a scam for publicity."

My stomach drops, and even though I perfectly heard what she said, I say, "What did you say?"

"He claims he has proof you're fake-dating Axl, and the photos he has posted are way different than the other ones you have. These look like you don't even know each other." A heavy sigh floats over the phone before she tacks on, "People will do anything to get their two minutes of fame."

"Right." I freeze, knowing how bad this will be if it gets outed as a scam. Axl and I would more than likely lose a majority of our fan bases. "Some people have the wildest ideas." My voice is flat as I try to sound as bored of this story as I can.

"In other news," Bailey goes on, "I know it's early for bad news, but I want to catch you before you get busy. I'm having a hard time rescheduling your concerts. I guess the venues don't want to take the risk, because your ticket sales weren't that great the first time."

"Oh really?" I scratch my cheek, replaying the inflections in her voice, searching for a hint of her leaving something out to protect me. "Did they say anything else? I do have a contract to perform there."

"No big announcement from either place. They both said their schedules were filled, which I understand being short notice. However, if we don't reschedule, we are looking at refunding ticket sales. That could cost the tour a lot of money. I'll have to talk to finance, but your ticket sales were down for most of this tour. I'm not sure you were that much money ahead to cover a huge payback like this."

"Well, aren't you the bringer of good news this morning?" I force a laugh to keep it light, but I don't feel light at all. I don't worry about my bank account, but I have a huge tour crew, and they all deserve to be compensated well. I had promised them profit-sharing bonuses if they stayed through the whole tour. If I have to pay back two whole concerts worth of tickets, I might not have the funds for bonuses, and that just stinks. Now, I'm too anxious to sit, and I slide off the bed, pacing up and down the narrow aisle by my bed.

"It'll be fine," Bailey says, lifting her tune. "I haven't given up on getting them rescheduled, just letting you know what I'm working on while you're off on romantic trips with your new hunk."

"Right." My jaw clenches as I force a breezy tone.

I'm so glad we aren't on FaceTime right now. This is not the news I need to hear. My tour lost all its profits, and my publicity-seeking stunt has already been outed as a scam. Great way to start the day.

"Well, have a safe flight, and I'll touch base later." Bailey's voice gets quieter with each word, as if she's pulling the phone away from her mouth.

"Bye." I doubt she hears me, because the line is already dead. I wrap my hand around my suitcase handle, tugging it out of the door. I'm glad we are leaving in the dark. I don't have it in me to fake this right now.

Apparently, my faking looks fake.

It's a lot harder than it looks.

Axl and I make it back to the plane without saying much of anything to each other. I want to ask if he knew about the news story, but I don't have the stomach to apologize for my failures right now. Once we get on the plane, it seems Axl has other plans than solitude. "He's a loser, you know."

"Pardon me?" I glance up from my phone and find him gazing at me with focus.

"Rocco. If that's why you're quiet." He gestures toward me with an open palm. "I just want you to know he doesn't deserve you. I hate seeing you so forlorn like this. Any guy would be lucky to even be in the same room as you."

Like you.

My eyes rocket wide open, and I'm so glad I didn't say that out loud. Somebody glue my mouth shut fast. "Er, thanks. Although, I'm definitely not thinking about *Rocco* anymore."

"Oh." He closes his mouth, and then opens it again. "I guess I was hoping, um, I mean, *thinking* that's why you were so quiet. Are you upset about something else?"

"No." I pause, sucking back air, preparing to explain how I ruined this for both of us, but as I open my mouth, he speaks first.

"I'm sorry I messed it up." He spikes a hand through his hair. "I don't get a lot of practice at this sort of thing, and last night I saw that photographer take our photo, and I tried to get it back, but it was too late."

"You didn't mess it up." Astonishment pools in my chest, as I can't believe he was thinking that. "I messed it up. I was so exhausted last night that I didn't even think about staying in character, and it was me who decided we needed to leave early. If we'd stayed with the plan, like *you* wanted to do, it would have been fine."

"It will be fine," he rushes but then stops talking abruptly when Skye appears from behind the curtain.

"Is there anything you need before takeoff?" She's already walking to the closest to get my usual.

"Yeah, pillow, blanket, and sparkling water," I rattle out, and then cut a glance back to Axl.

His gaze bounces from me to Skye. "I'll have what she's having." A small smile buds on his lips as he adds, "I might have gotten used to this. Too bad it's the last time."

"It doesn't have to be the last time." I take my pillow, placing it behind my head as I kick back my footrest and close my eyes.

"Sort of." His voice is somber. "I mean, I don't have a jet of my own, and I doubt you need a bad fake date tagging along with you."

I sputter out a laugh and open one eye. "Trust me, I enjoyed dating you."

What?

Why would I say that?

"What do you mean by that?" His voice takes an inquiring tone.

"I was wondering the same thing." I force a chuckle, trying to laugh it off, but I'm insanely curious about what I meant by that, too. "Maybe I just need some rest." I shut my eyes tight and pray he drops it.

"Maybe," he says in a definitive tone, and I hope he'll cut me some slack and drop my blunder.

Just don't say anything else. Let it go before I die.

"As far as fake dating goes," he says. His smirk sparking from the corners of his mouth. "I think we both know we're better off not."

"Right." My stomach drops, and I force myself to laugh. "Ha, ha . . ."

When we land in Mapleton, I need to recharge, and I couldn't be happier chilling at home. I hate that I had to cancel concerts to get these two weeks off, but it's been a long time since I had any breaks, and as each day passes at home, I can feel tension release a little more from my shoulders. I need a hard break.

However, it seems someone has other plans for me. I'm not home for more than an hour when there's a now familiar knock on the door. I know it's not Norma. Her knock is more persistent and tappy. This knock is measured and presuming.

I whip the door open and find Bill Baker standing where I had pictured him. His Granite Ice beanie covers his bald spot but emphasizes how unruly his eyebrows are, with long gray hairs spiking out from the center of the dark ones. It doesn't make him look unkept though, just more like a friendly grandpa, and I'm getting used to him.

"I saw your new photos." He clasps his hands behind his back, as if he's ready to give a speech. "People suspect you're faking this relationship."

"Yeah, I have no idea where those even came from." I wag my head back and forth. "I doubt anyone believes that story."

"I do," he asserts. "You two looked lost and unengaged. Not like a couple at all. We have to do something to change this fast, or we'll lose everything."

"I think it's time we admit we're defeated." I shrug, not willing to drag out this drama. "We can call it a rebound fling and say we both wish the best for each other, but neither one of us is ready for a relationship—"

"You need to kiss him," Bill blurts out.

Triple blinking, I'm stunned speechless, which grants Bill ample silence to explain, "You need to up your showmanship a little more. Give the people something to swoon over so they believe you're in love. Not those dopey expressions you had last night."

I just stand there, letting my jaw hang low and pondering how I'm going to explain this to him, but it's really not that hard. "Remember, we made a no-kissing pact."

"Everyone knows those are meant to be broken," he says quickly. "Listen, it's only going to work if you lay one on him when he's not expecting it. Otherwise, you'll both be too nervous, and it won't be believable. You're a natural actress and he's not. He'll clam up and ruin the moment."

"That is a violation." I wave my hands in a wide sweep in front of me. "I'm not going to throw myself on someone who I promised I wouldn't kiss."

"It's not a violation if he wants to," Bill goes on. "This fake-dating thing isn't working because you both know it's fake, but if one of you starts to believe it's real . . . then it won't look so stiff."

"What are you saying?" I mostly understand exactly what he's saying, but I ask because I'm making sure we're both having the same conversation. I had no idea Bill was so sneaky to even suggest I break the only rule we have.

"I'm saying, I want you to stop pretending like you're dating. It's not working. You two look awful together. Instead, I want you to start *dating* him for real."

I fold my arms, crossing them over my chest as Axl's comment on the plane about how we both know we would be bad at dating pulls to the front of my mind. Maybe he was fishing for my reaction? My little heart, which has been through so much these past few days, starts to pitter hard against my ribcage.

The thought of kissing Axl sends me into a place of bliss that I can't explain. The mere suggestion of his soft, full lips pressing against mine . . . I bite my lip to avoid smiling. I *love* the idea of it, but I don't think it's the best way to go about it. I'm not going to trick him into anything. If I ever kiss him, I want it to be for real. "This makes no sense."

"It will once you kiss him." His tone is easy, as if he's deciding to order toast with his over-easy eggs and not at all like he's running some scam.

"I'm not going to kiss him." I pause, but then decide to remind him about my morals. "Agreeing to pretend you are something in front of people you don't know is one thing, but Axl and I are friends now. Friends who agreed to not do certain things, and I'm not going to disrespect his boundaries."

"Where should it happen?" He rubs his facial stubble on his chin, ignoring my rebuttal as he plots out loud. "The date looked so staged at the fundraiser. People are also expecting a show at the arena, but what if . . ." His eyes slide over my front porch, and I visualize the wheels turning in his head.

"I don't think so." I throw up my hand in a stop motion. "This is a bad idea—"

"It's a perfect idea!" Excitement infuses his voice, and his smile spreads across his face. "It's the most believable setting. Invite him over to spend time with your family. That will get him thinking it's a genuine date, because it's not in public. There's no reason you'd ever have him over here unless you'd be interested in having some private time. Then maybe come out here to this nice porch to cuddle, and when things get cozy, you pucker up. I'll be hiding in those bushes with my camera."

"Absolutely not!" I shake my head violently. *Bill has lost his mind!* I recall when he first showed up on my porch and how I thought he was crazy then. He's only gotten crazier. He doesn't even have a normal setting. And how he comes up with these plans and voices them so easily makes me wonder what kind of business he's running. I don't know anything about owning a hockey team, but this isn't how people act. "Why would I do that to him? It's a breach of trust and so dishonest."

"I was hoping you'd ask that." Bill's eyes widen as he yanks his phone out of his back pocket and proceeds to open some app. "This morning was interesting," he narrates as he scrolls. "Not only did I see those photos of the two of you looking duller than

lead paint, but I saw something about how your tour is in trouble."
He flashes the article at me. "Do you know anything about this?"

My heart tanks from its already defeated position.

How did that get leaked?

After scanning the first few lines, it sounds as if a disgruntled
employee at one of the canceled venues leaked my lackluster ticket
sales and complained about my inability to reimburse the tickets
in a timely manner.

*Of course, there is no mention of my management trying to
reschedule the tour. They never mention any of the positive things I
do.*

"I know I can't believe everything I read online, but is this true?"
His eyes soften, smacking mine with a healthy dose of reality that
I've been avoiding since I talked to Bailey this morning.

"Some of it may be." Rolling my lips in, I contemplate how
much of my personal business to disclose to Bill, but he already
has more blackmail on me than any person on the planet. Maybe
he can help. He is a billionaire, after all. "We're trying to reschedule
the concerts, but they aren't even trying and are insisting on refunds. I don't want to do that, because my team deserves bonuses
for working so hard this last year. Most of them missed the whole
summer with their families."

"See, that's where we can help each other." Bill winks as he tucks
his phone into his back pocket. "We can make everyone happy if
we work together. Refund all the tickets, and instead of rebooking
at that venue, why not offer a free concert in a park or something?

People love that sort of stuff. You can say you're paying it forward for the inconvenience."

"I can't afford—"

"I can pay all their bonuses."

"Why would you do—" My brain catches up to my words and I freeze. "It will cost you a hundred grand to refund all those tickets. You think me kissing Axl is going to help that much?"

"I do." Bill rocks back on his heels, looking more confident than ever. "It saves face for this fake-dating rumor and restores hope for all our fans, which will fuel your career and the success of my team for years to come. I started this." He flashes a quick gaze to the ground. "I admit I didn't realize how clever the media would be, but we aren't done yet. Get a good kiss on camera. We can wait a few weeks for everyone to have a chance to believe in fairy tales, and then you can make your statement about not being ready to date. If we give up now, it fuels the story that it is all a farce."

"You sure love your hockey team, don't you?" I half chuckle, half wince. "This is an awful lot of trouble to go through to get fans, especially when you don't need the money."

"I may have my own bets to even." He winks at me, rocking back on his heels again.

"Oh really?" A veil lifts as it suddenly all makes sense as to why he's trying so hard. It's not about Axl or me. It's all about his ego. "Do tell?"

"Some secrets are better left secrets, but I'll say I may have made a bet—or two—about this team to some of my friends, and well, I don't like to lose." His smile spreads in a genuine grin, and he reaches out his hand. "What do you say? We help each other out one more time. One more act?"

I *hate* the idea of kissing Axl.

Wait, let's clarify.

I rather like the idea of kissing Axl, as I've been enamored with those lips since first glance. The part I hate is the deception, especially when we promised not to go there. Even if he allows it to happen, it's bound to massively confuse him. He's been nothing but a gentleman to me.

It's a terrible idea.

But if I don't do any damage control and allow these fake-dating rumors to fester, they could get out of hand, further sinking my career. I'll never make this tour money back. My crew could go unpaid, and the mere thought of that makes me want to hurl. Not to mention Axl's shot at the NHL goes down the drain.

I could make it a fast peck.

Sort of like a thank you.

As long as Bill gets it on camera.

Yeah, like a grandma kiss.

That could work.

A thank you and so long . . .

Oh, this is a terrible idea. I press my fingers to my temples, wishing I could bury all my problems, but they aren't going away. Bill is right. We started this. If we quit now, we look guilty. I already hate the words I'm about to say, but I take his hand in mine. "No promises. I'm not going to force myself on him, but if it feels like

I can slip one in there . . ." I roll my eyes as I can't believe what I'm saying. "I'll try."

He eagerly pumps my hand up and down. "You got yourself a pucker-up pact."

That's exactly what I'm afraid of. I drop his hand, mulling over how I'm going to get myself into this situation.

It has to be casual.

He can't suspect a thing.

Maybe I can make it like an accident where I fall on him.

Whatever it is, I have to come up with something quick before these rumors get out of hand.

Fourteen

Due to our morning travel, I missed early practice, but I'm not about to start making excuses. As soon as my feet hit solid ground, I drive over to the arena and run drills by myself. Truthfully, the time alone is cathartic and exactly what I need to clear my head. This whole thing with Sophie has my brain fogged up. Like, I fully understand she's only pretending to like me, but she's easy to hang out with, and last night at the charity ball, I wasn't expecting to feel so protective and even *jealous*.

When I looked at Rocco playing that game with her, all I thought about was putting my fist in his face, and the dude's never done anything to me. He became my poster child for every cheater, and I had a stirring in my gut that said it was time to get even.

Shaking my head, I skate off the ice after I'm done and head to the locker room. I slow as I round the corner, as by now, I half expect Bill Baker to be hiding in the shadows with another backroom deal. I let out a full sigh of relief when I find the boardroom empty.

Maybe he'll be happy now.

We did what we said we'd do.

Sophie and I can go about living our lives, and we'll make a breakup statement.

I stuff my stick in my bag and throw everything in my locker, as I have plans for another workout later tonight. After all, I'm not getting to the NHL by doing the minimum. I fish for my phone in my coat pocket and find a missed call from Sophie.

What does she want?

Our deal is done.

Why would she call and not text?

I hate that my mind immediately goes to Rocco. Assuming the worst, I don't hesitate to press call on her name. She answers on the second ring. "Hey, Axl." Her voice is cool and unstressed. That sends a wave of relief to my gut.

Not sure why I would have been stressed in the first place. "Hey." I breathe out and start to pace the hall. "I saw you called. Is everything okay?"

"Oh yeah," she quips. "Everything's great. I'm wondering . . . you know . . . everything was sort of a bustle these last few days. I know you're new to town and live by yourself, and my mom's making a meatloaf tonight, so I thought maybe you'd want a home-cooked meal."

Her words rush and garble at the end, but I hear her perfectly. Halting my steps, I stare at the blank wall before me.

She's literally inviting me to her parents' house for meatloaf. Why?

That is not part of the agreement.

"It's not a big deal if you're busy," she interrupts my scrolling thoughts. "I thought it might be nice to destress here, and I don't know . . . get to know each other better. There's no reason we can't hang out."

Getting to know each other is not part of the agreement.

Getting to know each other sounds like a date.

Why would she ask me on a date?

Unless?

"Hello?" Her voice takes on an inquiring tone. "Are you still there?"

"I'm here, but maybe." I want to say I'm confused, but I don't want to offend her. There's really nothing to be confused about. She's gorgeous. Any guy would jump at the chance to date her, including myself. I'm not lying to myself that aside from hockey, she's all I've been thinking about.

No confusion there.

It's just that we had an agreement to fake date, and I didn't want to be the one to break the agreement.

But . . . I tip my head to the side, as I think about this a little deeper. In our agreement to fake date, we never agreed not to date date.

I don't date. That's the rule I've had for myself.

But since we already had a fake date, it's sort of like I'm only half breaking my rule.

I mean, being new to town, I don't really know people to hang out with who aren't on the team, and I get enough of them. Plus, all they want to do is party in their free time, and I'm not a partier. Sophie and I get along well, and it would give me something to do.

Back to my no-dating rule. It's been a strict rule I've kept since I was seventeen. I didn't even break it in college, when I had my teammate trying to set me up with every other hot single chick they saw. I've been so focused on hockey that I've never even wanted to break my no-dating rule.

Sophie . . . she's so different than other girls I've met. It's not just about how sensationally gorgeous she is, but being with her is so easy. You'd never know she was famous. She is just a super chill chick.

But if she wanted to go on a date, she wouldn't ask me to a family dinner. More than likely she's just bored being in Mapleton and wants to hang out. I'm sure that's it, and there's nothing wrong with chilling. "Ah, yeah. S-sure," I finally stammer, finding my verbal bearings. "I think that sounds great. Is there anything I can bring?"

"Mom's taking care of dinner, but if you want to find a wine for us for later, that might be nice."

Since I'm always in training mode, I never drink, but if a pretty girl asks me to bring the wine, of course I'm going to bring it. "Consider it done."

"Good." Her voice smooths even more as she confirms the details. "How about six?"

"I'll be there."

"Great. See you then." She ends the call, and I stare at her name blinking on my phone, and my fingers tingle.

I don't have a clue in the world what just happened.

I'm also not a fan of meatloaf, but I'm too curious to skip it.

My heart flops ungracefully like a hippo doing a belly flop, and I feel the aftershocks wave out through my extremities.

I'm going on a date with my fake date tonight.

I hope this doesn't mess things up.

Fifteen

Sophie

Taking a deep breath, I straighten the hem of my wool sweater and stare at my reflection in my bedroom mirror. I still look like the same girl who left this small town five years earlier with all those hopes and dreams. Even though so much has changed, I still feel like the same old me that used to sleep in this room every night.

The room hasn't changed much at all, either. My mom kept the matching white-wicker furniture, complete with a papasan chair. That was all the rage when I was in school, and I couldn't believe I got one, making all my friends jealous. I spent hours curled up on that thing, writing song lyrics—most have never been sung out loud. For good reason of course. Most were horrible. But I kept at it, dreaming my dream so hard I'd get stomach aches that kept me up all night, and eventually things paid off.

It's funny how coming back home for a few days has me thinking about all the things, but one thought is new: Axl.

I'd only known him for a couple of weeks, but I'm no longer surprised when I find myself thinking about him. I'm looking forward to seeing him tonight—not because I told Bill I'd try to kiss him—but because I'm a little bored hanging out around the house. I used to spend so much time with Rocco. Now there's this void of time I'm not sure what to do with. Axl fills it nicely, and I certainly haven't shed even one tear over Rocco since I met Axl.

"Hey, Twinkie!" The voice of my brother, Sam, is followed by disorganized pounding on my door. Hearing my childhood nickname slams me back to simpler days when my life's purpose was to score an extra dessert in my lunch box. I've always had a sweet tooth.

Flinging my door open, I point a harsh finger at Sam. "Don't call me that in front of Axl."

"Whatever you say, Twinks. Oh, and he just pulled up in a truck." In a flash, he whisks his hand to his back pocket and springs a water gun on me. Knowing exactly what he's up to—because we had this duel out every day for years—I drop to the floor, roll across the hall into the bathroom, and slam the door, only getting sprayed in the leg a little. An amused grin laces my lips as I tiptoe to the closet and dig in the back of the towel stack—way up under the big ugly towels Mama used to dye her hair— to find the gun I'd hidden back when I was in high school.

"Did you hear me?" Sam calls from the other side of the door. "I said your guest is here."

"I'm not falling for that." I fill my gun under the faucet, and my gaze slides to the tiny bathroom window. It's tempting but I doubt I can crawl out of it. It's awfully high off the ground and not that big. With my luck, I'll get stuck and my parents would do something insanely embarrassing like calling the fire department.

I don't need that headline.

"He's walking up the porch," Sam calls out, his voice sounding so close, I bet his face is smeared up against the door.

"I said I'm not falling for that." I secure the plug in my canister and pump the double barrels full of water. He knows not to test me. I've held out in this bathroom for over two hours before. It won't take long, and he'll give up, walking away. The creaky wood floors will tip me off when that happens. I'll wait until he's all the way down the hall and then I'll bust out, barrels blazing. My shoulders bounce as I suppress a giggle.

Who does he think he is?

I invented this game.

I crouch near the door and hold my breath as I press my ear closer. It only takes a moment, and the whole thing plays out like clockwork, like I knew it would. First, there's the creak of the floorboard directly across from this door, and then two more seconds and he pads over the creaky board in front of the laundry room. In only four more steps, he's all the way down the hall, so I only wait two seconds before I spring up with full force, whip open the door, and open fire.

I got him!

Just where I knew he'd be.

At the end of the hall standing in front of the foyer. I pump more water into my gun as I run toward him, hollering like I'm on an ambush squad. "Surrender!"

The oddest thing happens.

He doesn't pull his gun back up to shoot, and he doesn't run. He turns his face to me . . . and I die. So much blood rushes to my face that I get dizzy.

Not Sam.

It's Axl, and I've drenched him. One of my feet slides back, as I entertain the idea of running into the bathroom and refusing to come out. *Why did Sam set me up like that?*

Little brothers are the worst.

Sam and my parents stand slack-jawed in the adjacent kitchen, laughing like a pack of hyenas.

"I'm so sorry," I say, struggling to know what to do. I should run back and grab a towel for him, but I should also take a minute to explain why I was acting like a feral ten-year-old boy. "I thought you were my brother."

His lips bend slowly, as if he's testing to make sure the attack is over. It's the first glimpse that he's not going to be mad at me. "I understand . . .?" His statement comes out like a question, and my cheeks flame with massive rage at Sam for putting me in this situation.

"I'll grab a towel for you." I spin on my heel in a hustle to the bathroom when an entire gulf stream of *freezing* water blasts my back. I scream, so confused. One glance over my shoulder confirms that Axl's in on it!

He's pulled a gun out from somewhere, and he's firing this way!

How did that happen? Sam must have got to Axl first and set this whole thing up.

I'm laughing and screaming all the way back to the bathroom. Once again, I slam the door as a barrier. I grab two towels, wrapping one around myself, and crack the door open, calling out, "Okay, you won. We need to call a truce before the parents get mad."

"Truce." There's nothing sus in his tone, and I peek my head out. His gun sits on the floor at the end of the hall, and he's walking toward me. "Would you believe me if I said Sam made me do that?"

"Actually, I do believe you." I push the door open all the way, and throw a towel at him, fully seeing he got soaked much worse than I did, "This is his thing." I drag the towel over the puddles on the floor. "I see you already met everyone." I motion to the chorus of snickering still piping out from my parents in the kitchen. As I turn back, it's obvious to both Axl and me that a towel isn't going to dry him off. "I'm so sorry. Dad," I say, raising my voice, trying to cut through the laughter rushes. "Can you lend Axl a shirt?"

Dad rises to his feet, every smile line on his face deepening as he ushers Axl back to his room, and I'm left standing in the hall. "Sam," I murmur under my breath. "I'm going to change, and when I get back out here, remind me to kill you."

His laughter calls my bluff, and I'm not chuckling as I playfully glare at him. He's not even wet. His dark hair lies perfectly against his head, and his gamer T-shirt looks like it just came out of the dryer. As much as Sam can be sooo annoying, I'm oddly grateful for this distraction. My nerves about kissing Axl have calmed and everyone is laughing. It's not how I *expected* this introduction to go, but the ice is clearly broken.

Sixteen

I feel uncomfortable as Sophie's dad takes me back to his room, but I hum in my head to get through it. He's chatty, telling me his name is Shawn. Apparently, everyone in this family has S names, with her mom being Susan. That's cute. I'm sure he's sending me a subliminal message when he hands me a T-shirt from his closet that says, "Dads Against Daughters Dating." The word *dating* is in one of those warning circles with an X over it. Good thing we are only fake dating. I can't help but tease a grin and say, "Thanks."

I return to the kitchen, and Sophie's still sputtering out little rushes of laughter. "I'm so sorry. I had no idea you were here."

"It's only water." I chuckle, still seeing the image of her shocked expression in my head. That was priceless. Everything I expected it to be and more. She's just one of those chill girls that's easy to hang out with.

"Thanks, bruh." Sam reaches over for a high-five. "That was so fire!"

I smack his hand, strangely feeling like we're part of some club. "You're welcome, *bruh*." I've never been up on Gen Z lingo, but it's sort of fun to pretend to know what it means. Plus, bruh feels good to say. It hangs in your throat and sounds tough.

"Dinner is ready," Susan calls from the kitchen as she's busy setting the salad and potatoes on the table. All the food is dished into matching white tableware and looks very inviting."

Sophie leads me to the modest wood table in the center of the kitchen, and we all shuffle around it, filling the seats. "I feel like we're doing this backwards, seeing as how you met everyone already. I'm sorry I didn't get to the door when you came. I honestly didn't hear the doorbell."

"I didn't ring it." I laugh again, recalling how it all went down. "I pulled up to the house, and right away I saw the bushes moving. I thought it was a raccoon, but it was awfully animated."

"The bushes were moving?" Sophie's face stills and her eyes widen. She must have anxiety about these kinds of things. "Huh, did you see anyone—I mean any*thing*?"

"Yeah, it was your brother. He was waving me closer to tell me his plan."

"It was only Sam." Sophie's eyes shift side to side before she tacks on, "You didn't see anybody else?"

It was my turn to shift my eyes side to side. "Was I supposed to find someone else?"

"No," she blurts out and then rushes to add, "I mean, it's just weird. Sort of *scary* to think about someone hiding in the bushes." She elbows her brother. "Glad it was just you, Sam."

Sophie must have some phobia of being snuck up on or something, because her entire facial expression has changed. Maybe living with a brother who is always starting water fights makes her paranoid?

"Anyway." Shawn clears his throat as he passes the potatoes to me. "Glad you could visit us tonight. We don't get to see much of Sophie anymore, and it's rare she brings a guy home."

I scoop out the potatoes and pass them to Sophie. "Thank you for having me. It's been a long time since I had a home-cooked meal."

"If you're excited about the food," Shawn replies, "you can rest assured Susan's meatloaf is not only above average, but it's the some of the best you'll ever eat."

I steal a gaze at Sophie, who's beaming back at both of her parents. Their energy all syncs together, creating this harmony, nothing like what happens at my parents' house. I have a happy family, but both my parents have solid careers, and they work a lot. We ate dinner together when they were home, but they were mostly quiet. My parents sure didn't allow water guns in the house. I would have been grounded for life for that. I got grounded for a whole month when I put a puck through the basement door. They were so particular with their décor and keeping things nice. Not that there's anything wrong with treating things with respect, but they could stand to loosen up a bit.

Once the food is all circulated, Shawn takes his wife's hand and bows his head. It's obvious he's going to pray, and I follow his lead and lower my gaze, half wondering if this is going to be another joke.

"Dear Lord," Shawn recites with what seems like sincere commitment, "thank you for this food, for those who prepared it, and for the family and our new friend, Axl, with whom we share it. In Jesus' name, we pray. Amen." He raises his gaze back to his plate, and everyone digs in as if it's the most natural thing in the world.

I'm quite honored he included my name in his prayer. I don't come from an overly spiritual background. I've been to church and all, but my family never prayed in front of strangers. I dig into my meatloaf, and it only takes a couple of bites for me to agree with Shawn that Susan's meatloaf is *above average.* It's not only seasoned to perfection but has amazing chew through, but in the oddest way, it's not the meatloaf that makes this meal amazing. If I must explain it, I'll say it's because of the company making me feel so welcome.

"So, Axl." Susan sort of hums from her seat across from me. "Tell us about yourself. Where did you grow up, and what's your family like? Have you always played hockey?"

"Certainly." Swallowing my food, I straighten my spine and fix my gaze on her. "I grew up in the Midwest. Only child. Two great parents. Dad is a milk hauler, and my mom is a nurse who works nights. The town I'm from has only about five hundred people, and there's not much to do, especially in winter. I would usually spend my time on the pond ice skating since it was free and by my house. I didn't even know I was good at it until our middle school formed a hockey team. The coach had seen me skating at the park and asked me to try out. After that, everything became about hockey. I got lucky and was able to play in college, where we made it to the championship games in our division. That game was televised, and that's how Bill Baker, the owner of Granite Ice, saw me. He flew out and offered me a spot as a starter for his new team."

"That worked out pretty smoothly." Susan beams at me. "Have you been to Mapleton before?"

"Never heard of it." I chuckle, remembering that I didn't even remember where Vermont was on the map.

"Do you like it so far?" Susan asks as she takes a bite of potatoes.

"Yeah, it's not too bad." I saw off a chunk of my meatloaf.. "I'm used to small towns. As long as I have a place to sleep and skate, I'm happy."

"Well," Shawn interjects, holding his finger up as his elbow rests on the table, "I will tell you two secrets nobody knows about this town unless you're born and raised."

I steal a gaze at Sophie. She's happily chewing her food, and something about seeing her doing the most normal thing stirs my heart. It feels special to be included in this part of her life. I would have never expected this, but just sitting next to her at the dinner table makes it really hard to focus on Shawn. I slide my lips over my teeth, and I lean toward Shawn. "What are the secrets?"

"The first happened years ago." Shawn starts off with the utmost serious expression on his face. I half expect a ghost story, so I'm swallowing and tuning in. "A circus was driving through town and crashed along the interstate overpass. All their monkey cages were dumped, and the monkeys escaped into the brush. People thought they'd all die off in the New England weather, but surprisingly, they've been populating and carrying on with their best lives. So, if you ever notice any wild monkeys, it's not your imagination."

Thinking he's joking, I start to chuckle, but everyone holds their serious expression, so I swallow my humor. "Wow, that's crazy. I haven't seen anything like that, but thanks for the heads up."

"This one's even better," he says, letting me in on the second secret. "When I was growing up, there was a huge media kerfuffle in the local papers about someone breaking into a barn and 'spooking' some chickens. It was a regular thing, where every morning there was another complaint that Farmer Hanson's barn was being broken into. This was well before video cameras were a thing, so we had to set a good ol' fashion stakeout to stay up all night and see what was going on. Turns out, his rowdy son was running an illegal casino underneath the barn! He'd dug himself a root cellar with a trap door he covered with a big pile of hay, and he was entertaining travelers from all over, but . . . " Shawn pauses and wags his finger at me. "The best part is that these travelers were usually hungry, and Farmer Hanson's son learned how to cook. With a lack of resources, he grilled steak kebobs over an open camp fire. Of course, they were breaking every fire code there ever was, but those were the best cuts of meat a man will ever eat." He licks his lips as if he can still taste the kabobs. "When they came to shut down the casino, those kebabs won over the police. Somehow, he got off with some phony ticket and a business license to set up his own kabob shop right in the town square—"

"Wait a second," I interrupt as I'm putting two and two together. "You're not telling me that's where Red Barn Kebobs in town square got their start, are you?"

"I knew your mama didn't raise a fool." Shawn's smile spreads wide as he chuckles at his own joke. "Isn't that wild?"

"It's true." Sophie nods as her eyes sparkle back at me. I am thoroughly engrossed in this story, but it doesn't stop me from noticing how stunning Sophie is, even when she's doing the most mundane things, like eating average meatloaf. "They do have the *best* kebobs," she gushes. "Have you tried them yet?"

"No, I haven't. I've only seen the sign, but now that I know it's famous history, I'll have to go there." An idea sparks in my head, and before I have a chance to push it away, I risk it. "Maybe you and I can check it out together?"

Her eyes drop to her plate. Her lashes flutter a few times before she raises her gaze back to mine. "Yeah, that's definitely something we can plan on."

"Well." Shawn pushes his chair back as he takes the napkin off his lap and sets it on his plate. "That meatloaf was delicious like always. Thanks for dinner, honey."

"Don't get up yet. I was just going to bring out my famous boiled eggs." Susan stands and motions for us to stay sitting.

Sophie nearly sprays water out of her mouth from the cup she was drinking out of. "No eggs, Mama, but thanks."

Susan laughs as well, collecting plates. I had been so entranced in Shawn's stories, I hadn't noticed everyone had cleaned their plates, including myself.

"Yes, thank you." I stand, lifting my plate and carrying it to the sink. "Can I help with anything?" "You are welcome." Susan comes up from behind me, lowering her stack of dishes to the counter. "It sounds sort of corny, but doing dishes is sort of my me time. I turn on my Loretta Lynn and we just vibe." She nods toward Sophie. "You two kids can just relax. I know it's been a long time since Sophie has had time off."

"I agree. And I have an idea." Sophie slides in next to her mom, reaches into the cupboard, and retrieves two glasses and a corkscrew. She motions to the bottle of wine I brought that's still resting untouched on the counter. "We can take that wine on the porch. It's screened in, and a little chilly, but if we take a blanket, it might be cozy." She winks at me, and a zap of electricity slams into my gut.

I understood her being neighborly and inviting me over for a home-cooked dinner after we'd become friends and all, but *wine on the porch* feels awfully like a date to me.

The thing is, there's a magnetic pull from me directly to Sophie that pulsates, telling me that I want to have wine on the porch with her. "Yeah, let's do that."

I grab the wine, and she snatches up a heavy throw blanket from the sofa, and we head out to the front porch, taking a seat on the wood swing in the corner. The swing creaks when it pulls back, but it's nothing we can't ignore. I don't protest when she offers me half of the blanket and we spread it over both our laps. It's chilly, but not past the point of comfort, and if anything it just gives us an incentive to sit close.

She swaps her smile from the one that was vibrant, full of life, and teasing to something more secret, that she hasn't shared with me before.

It's flirty and languid.

Beautiful.

Directed at me.

And so, so confusing!

There's not a soul in sight. No reason for us to act like we're a couple, yet her smile is more a genuine *I'm-interested-in-you* smile than anything she's given me thus far.

She sets about removing the cork from the wine, and I take the glasses and hold them out for her. After she fills each glass, she folds her half of the blanket over, and leans way forward to place the bottle on the porch, then leans back on the porch swing, and snuggles even closer to me. Her eyes pace between my face to the bushes behind us. After catching her staring at the bushes a second time, I get paranoid. "Is there something in there you're seeing?" I look around but she quickly drops her hand to *my leg!*

"Oh, no!" she blurts out. "Just watching the wind blow through the leaves." She leans closer, bringing a waft of her scent right into my airway. It's the smell of honey and vanilla. Her voice lowers to a sultry tone, and she whispers, "Tell me about this wine," right as she takes a sip.

"I don't really know anything about it. I grabbed the bottle that was on sale." Her eyes lock on mine, sending pulsating spirals, and I get the impression she has something rather specific in her mind. She takes the glass from my hand and sets it alongside hers on the floor next to the wine bottle. Her gaze flickers to my mouth and back to my eyes. All her facial features soften as she bites down on her bottom lip while a little giggle leaks from her lips.

It's clear she wants me to kiss her.

My mind flashes back to our no-kissing rule, and I at once disregard that as a boundary that was placed for our acting, and we clearly *aren't* performing right now.

Something is building between us, some sort of electromagnetic chemistry.

I don't have one doubt that I could kiss her and get away with it, despite the pact, but it feels sort of *rushed*.

This whole date seems *rushed*, and with the way she's looking at me, I can tell she's interested, but she did just have a public breakup. Maybe this is more about her being lonely than wanting to be with me. It's one thing to be a fake date, but I'm not going to be somebody's rebound guy.

Yet, she smells so so so—

"Call me crazy." She reaches out, playfully tracing a finger on my chin. "I just have the sudden urge to kiss you."

My breath hitches. *There's no misreading that.* My heart motors against my ribcage, and racing thoughts funnel through my mind. *Kiss me, being the loudest one.* "Doesn't that break the pact?"

"It does," she whispers, the pads of her fingers still intact on my chin. "Is that okay if I promise it won't change anything? It's just a fun kiss."

A frantic flutter slams into my heart, nearly halting it.

There's no such thing as a fun kiss. Not in my book. I've done the heartbreak thing before, and it's too powerful to mess around with this stuff. I'm not about to be someone's toy. But . . . if she has another idea, one that means we break the pact because we both feel this chemistry pulling us together, then I can go with that.

"You can kiss me." I place my hand on her hand that's still securely holding my leg. I may not be able to diagnose what sparked this urge of hers, but one thing I know is if I kiss her, she's mine.

There'll be no more games.

"But if you do," I say, lowering my voice into a warning, "it changes *this whole thing*. We can't circle back to a talking stage, and I don't do situationships that neither of us understand. No more faking it.

If you kiss me, *you're mine*."

Her eyes waver for a mere moment, back to my lips, before hooking on mine again. Goosebumps dot my spine as the puck is in her possession. One tiny kiss gives me permission to claim her, and I wait patiently for her to either agree or disagree to the new terms.

Her eyelids close at the slowest speed, and she is unwavering in yield to me.

I cup her cheek in the palm of my hand, letting my fingers brush below her ears, and even though I'm sitting, my knees buckle.

Instinctively my eyes close when our lips bond together, and I plummet into her warmth. My heart drums against my chest, wringing my breath out from me.

Ruining me as I'm completely willing to chuck my no-dating rule out the door.

Blending her and me—

Achoo!

We startle, at once pulling apart, our gazes slamming to the giant bush next to us. "Did that bush just sneeze?" I choke out, barely able to make audible words as my lips have completely gone numb from the tingles she left me with.

"Not the bush." She jolts to her feet, wrapping her hand fast around my wrist and yanking me off the swing. "It's . . . it's the *wild monkeys,* and we have to get inside right away!" She pulls me forward at top speed, knocking over the glasses of wine, and I don't have a chance to have a closer look.

After yanking open the door, she tugs me through it while pulling it shut behind us. We're left tangled together, and I fall back against the door, breathless. I don't have a clue what happened but the living room's dark now. Her parents have likely gone to their room. The only light is the flicker of the porch light coming in at an angle through the front picture window. The light shadows dance across her face, dusting gold tendrils across her flawless skin.

I'm doomed.

I drop my hand on her hip, drawing her to me, and I take my other hand, wrapping it into hers. My hand completely eclipses her petite palm, and I'm acutely aware of all the ways our skin brushes together between each finger.

I don't know what we just escaped outside.

I don't think I believe in that wild monkey story.

But wild monkey or not, I'm not letting her avoid what just happened. I lift her hand to my mouth, press my lips onto the top of her knuckle, and imprint a kiss before I repeat, "You just changed the whole thing."

Seventeen

Sophie

My lower jaw quivers as I crawl under my down comforter, hugging it tightly around my shoulders. My mind whirlwinds through all the emotions.

Confusion.

Sooo guilty, yet so swept off my feet.

Breathless.

More confused.

I honestly don't know what happened!

I had a plan. It was strategic. A quick, almost funny kiss that I could blame on the wine tomorrow.

The plan didn't stick.

When our gazes synced, my emotions *emotioned hard*, and I wasn't pretending. Everything that happened in those three minutes on the porch was real—well, minus the wild monkeys, but how else was I going to explain a sneezing bush? Moses wouldn't have believed it either.

Now, I'm wrecked.

I'm so conflicted because even though the kiss was genuine, the terms by which it started are so *wrong*. This is not a proper way to start a . . . thing? Whatever this is?

Do I tell him I had a little encouragement from Bill to kiss him?

Oh, no! I swipe a hand over my forehead, flushing at that idea. *I can't tell him that!*

But the money?

Yeah, I shake my head back and forth, even though no one can see it. There's no way I'm taking the money. I'm so embarrassed I ever considered it.

But my tour crew won't get a bonus.

My mind is a ping-pong match, pulling me in all directions.

I guess . . . I work harder to get the money from somewhere else. Maybe delay the bonuses?

They will understand that, right?

I'm sure that will be fine.

But then back to Axl.

Does he have to know I tricked him?

I dig my teeth into my bottom lip, but that only makes me remember how it felt to have our lips tangled together. Kissing him was everything I imagined and so much more. The way his soft lips folded into mine, tucking and pulling in the gentlest way.

When I close my eyes, I can almost feel it happening all over again, and I never want to forget this feeling.

I faceplant into my pillow and suppress a scream. Part of me wants to squeal like a middle school girl who just had her first kiss but the other part...is so disappointed I didn't do better.

What do I do now?

I wake up early and barely have one eye open when I spot a text from Axl flashing on my phone.

AXL: Good morning, beautiful.

So much guilt tsunamis over me while all the butterflies flutter to gather in my gut.

How can I experience two polar-opposite emotions at the same time? I cringe. Rocco and I dated for two years, and he never sent me a sweet good-morning text like that. How can this super sweet guy be right in front of my face this whole time, but *I missed him* until I've went too far?

I want to text back, letting him know I'm thinking about him, that I haven't stopped thinking about him, and if I add any more thoughts to the already humongous pile of thoughts, my head will explode. As much as I'm ready to put all this fake dating behind me, there's a niggling in the back of my head that says you have *one chance* to be honest before it gets out of hand. It's a mere misunderstanding now. Fix it before it blows up and you destroy any real shot you have to be together.

I stare at my phone.

I mean . . . that's so lame to say all that, especially in a text message.

He understands all the fake-dating stuff already.

Most of it.

I hug my pillow tightly against my chest, as if it has the power to help me come up with a solution. I weigh my options. Even if I do tell him everything, it's best not to tell him over a text. Instead of blabbering out my confession, I play it safe.

Me: Good morning. You're up early.

Axl: I get up at five to practice . . . gotta be there two hours before everyone else.

Axl: But it's not like I slept. I kept thinking about our kiss.

Giving up, I drop my phone and facepalm my forehead. He wasn't kidding that everything changed. He's not even pretending to be cool about his feelings. I take another breath, but it does nothing to cleanse the quakes in my stomach.

Me: I've been thinking about you, too.

Almost simultaneously another text comes back.

Axl: I want to see you. Can you come to our home game tonight?

I'm about to type *yes,* when I pause and remember Bill saying he didn't want us to have any more public appearances. But he didn't really mean I couldn't come. He meant he needed something else to prove our relationship, right?

I want to go.

There's no reason for me not to go.

Everyone already thinks he's my boyfriend.

Before I find another reason to doubt anything, I text back.

Me: I'll be there.

Axl: All right, now that's settled. I still want to see you. How about lunch? Red Barn Kebobs. I'll pick you up.

As much as I love seeing him on ice, the whole public charade still scares me a little, but kebabs are totally my language. It's an easy place to have lunch, and so perfect because it will give me a chance to be honest with him. Hopefully, he'll laugh it off, and we'll be able to move on, leaving this mess behind us.

Me: I'll be ready whenever you are.

I take my time getting dressed, loving this whole change of pace lifestyle of being in Mapleton. As a teenager, I was in such a hurry to bust out of this place, hoping to make my mark on the world, that I never took the time to appreciate it. I tug on a bright pink sweater with a boatneck and adjust it several different ways. I've never been the girl to be able to wear a one-shoulder sweater and actually look poised. After years of having people dress me, I learned a few tips, one being that no matter what you wear, have at least one thing that you love. That enjoyment will elevate your mood, and that will overflow to your confidence.

Today, I need all of the confidence I can get. Pink is my favorite color—always has been and always will be—and I'm wearing pink in confidence.

Leaving my hair down, it falls naturally into beachy waves. I run a brush through it but don't fuss any further. I know I'm about to meet Axl—the trembles in my palms tell me that much over and over—but I don't have any desire to get overly made up. Maybe it's because we're going to a place called Red Barn, but I am ready to be regular me.

After making my way out to the porch, I sit on the swing, letting the tips of my toes graze the deck as I playfully move the swing back and forth. The memory of last night is on a big screen in my head. It doesn't take long before Axl's blue truck comes barreling down our narrow dirt road, crawling to a stop right in front of Bill's bush. I bite back a giggle as I recall the sneeze.

That could have gone so badly!

Who would have guessed my dad's wild monkey story would ever come in handy?

Axl jumps out of his truck, and I run to meet him. As we narrow the gap between us, I slow my steps, feeling a pause. Axl said something last night that made my heart squeeze tight, and I'm unsure if things might be awkward today. He doesn't slow his stride, taking me right into a giant bear hug. I smile like I've never smiled before as he presses a kiss to my forehead, inhales deeply, and whispers, "You smell amazing."

"You might be having those kabobs on the brain a little too much." He snickers at my joke, but I don't join him. I should be celebrating with all the fizzy bubbles of a new crush, but instead I'm flooding with guilt. The way his eyes graze over me with such pride, I wish I would have done what my gut told me to do and called Bill first thing this morning. I didn't because I couldn't be sure he wasn't at the rink. I trust he's careful about things, but I can't risk Axl overhearing anything. I need to make sure when we do talk it's private.

"Is there anything you need to warn me about these kabobs?" He laces his fingers between mine, and we stroll slowly down the drive, stealing glances at each other every other step.

"No, they're fantastic, despite the scandalous origin story. Since they're cooked over an open flame, most of the fat drips off, making them surprisingly healthy." We arrive at the passenger side of the pickup, where he opens my door and reaches around, placing a hand on my hip. I assume he's going to help me into his truck since it's awfully high up, but instead he spins me around and slowly pushes me until my feet glide all the way back against the side of his truck. He playfully secures me there with his hand still on my hip. Not wasting a second to move in, he places his other hand on my chin and lowers his mouth until his roguish smile hovers over me, but neither of us move. We're so close, that I can see each tiny dot where his whiskers were recently shaved, and even a few uncreased smile lines that don't deepen with his usual smile. There's a glint of excitement in the corner of his eyes, causing exhilaration to barrel into my chest. My emotions clog my throat, and all that pressure makes me feel as if my chest is about to cave in at any moment.

I've never had anyone look at me like this before, but I can't take in the moment with this massive secret. My lips quiver as I test out words of confession. Before I can get anything out, he lowers his lips to mine, extending them into the sweetest of tender kisses, which becomes my undoing.

Kissing him is a reset button—a hard reset that wipes all my thoughts instantly, and the only thing that matters is the now. He and I and whatever this is, it all molds together so beautifully.

When he pulls away, his gaze dances over my face before he upgrades his smile to one that's more feral. Before I know what's going on, he scoops me up and places me in the truck. I force my jaw not to hang too low.

He's treating me like a princess. This is the man I've dreamed of my whole life, and I'm ruining this moment with these obsessive thoughts. I need to tell him about the money, and hopefully we can laugh it off.

The sooner, the better.

It's like ripping off a Band-Aid.

"Axl." My voice is small but not weak. "I want to get some—"

"Hey." A voice echoes from the porch. I cut a quick glance in that direction, but I already know it's Sam, and he almost always has a water gun. "Where are you two sneaking off to?"

"Get in the truck!" I scream, grabbing Axl's wrist, and yanking. *I could kill Sam right now for interrupting us. Just one time I would like a little privacy!*

Axl seems confused but eventually gives in and helps me pull him inside, rolling right over the top of me to find the driver's seat. I slam my door as fast as I can before pounding my finger on the automatic lock button, trapping us inside. "Sorry." I puff out waves of laughter as I try to get in a deep breath. "I didn't mean to become unhinged on you, but Sam always has a water gun."

Axl tips his head back, and a deep belly laugh rolls out. He casually reaches behind his seat. It looks like a stretch at first.

That's what I tell myself.

A little odd.

But hockey players are insanely flexible.

Suddenly, my heart slams against my chest, and I jump as he whips out a giant water gun. "You mean like this one?" His grin is savage as he blasts me at point-blank range, and I shrink, grappling for the door handle, but it's locked! I take too long to find the lock before I practically fall out of the truck and race to the house.

But there's Sam at his post from the front step, and he has a long barrel gun with serious range.

And he's in on it too!

It's insanity that these two guys have only known each other for less than twenty-four hours, and they've already teamed up against me. *I never expected that.* I'm without ammo and options, and I throw up my hands. "You guys fight unfairly. I give up!"

Axl jogs back down the drive, laughing so hard he's about to drop to his knees. Sam's snickering from the step, his gun hanging at his side.

"How did you guys even coordinate this?" I bristle, swiping my gaze from one perpetrator to the other, not sure what way I should walk as I am in the middle of the driveway.

It's Sam's turn to speak up, revealing how conniving he is. "I saw your phone on the counter this morning with a text from Axl."

"You looked at my phone!" My jaw drops, and I'm once again reminded how annoying little brothers can be. "Those are private conversations."

"Then maybe you should have a different password than your birthday."

"Shh!" Frantically waving, I try to cover his blurting. It's no use, and my words fall into laughter, as I know he's right. "I guess so," I mutter, pretending to be hurt. I throw my hand back up, tossing a glance back to Axl, both our smiles still beaming, "Now what? We are back where we were last night. It's too cold to walk around in wet clothing. Both of us need a change of clothes, and our plans for food are thwarted."

His brows bead together. "Why do you say that?"

"You need to get to the arena for pregame warmups. Do you have time to wait for me to change and still drive all the way to town?"

"This is where you underestimated my strategizing." He wags a playfully cocky finger in my direction as he takes a step back. "I already grabbed the kabobs on my way over here. I have them in the truck, and I bought enough for everyone."

My lips fall apart, revealing my surprise. "You did?"

"Yeah." He takes another step backwards toward his truck. "Figured it was my turn to treat." He pivots around, striding to his truck, and as I watch him, my heart flutters little baby flutters that whisper, *This guy can't be for real*.

It's one thing to have chemistry.

It's another thing to be able to be playful and laugh until your stomach hurts.

But finding a man who fits in with my family . . .

Axl Erikson, you just stole a hockey-puck-sized piece of my heart.

Eighteen

Axl

The kebobs were worth all the hype. I stayed at Sophie's house for hours after lunch, doing nothing more than sitting around her living room, snuggling on her couch, telling jokes with Sam, and listening to Shawn tell more of his small-town whoppers. I can't tell if those stories are real or not, but ever since last night, I've been considering being a little more cautious when I cut through the arena parking lot.

I arrive at pregame warmups on time, which is late for me. It leaves me unsettled, but I shake it off and change. Now, I'm laced up and standing in the tunnel with the guys, waiting for our cue to go out for warmups.

Holding my extra jersey, I adjust it, rolling it over in my hands. I've never even let another woman touch one of my jerseys before. I know it's early, but I won't be able to stand looking at Sophie sitting out there without my brand. My mind keeps replaying the day, and if I close my eyes and inhale, I can still smell her, honey with spicy undertones that didn't take me long to become obsessively addicted to.

I just want to be near her, and if I can't, she's going to be wearing my number. The music starts, and we skate out. The crowd is thunderous like never before. I scan the arena. Every seat is filled, and the fans are on their feet. My gaze is calculated as I peruse the owner's box for Sophie.

She's not there.

I sweep the arena, frantically seeking her, and my smile returns when it lands on her sitting by the player's bench.

Right where she belongs now.

I skate over to her, my heart ticking hard against my rib cage, as I wait for her eyes to lock on me. When they do, my heart nearly misses a beat. I reach my jersey over the Plexiglass while holding my breath. I know she's not a huge hockey fan, but I hope she understands the gesture. I considered waiting to give it to her in private, but there's nothing private about this relationship, and I want the whole world to know *she's mine.*

Her gaze wavers from the jersey to my eyes while her perfectly pouty lips slide into a brilliant smile, and she stands, taking it from me. The crowd screams a high-pitched swoony squeal, and I'd be lying if I said it didn't make my toes curl when she slipped the jersey over her head.

Man, she looks good in a jersey.

I'm not one to fall for this romantic stuff, but everything about Sophie makes this natural.

She's mine.

The female squeals in the crowd become unhinged. I drown them out because there's only one voice I need to tune in to. Besides, it's time *to skate.*

Hockey is always fast, but tonight's game is sloppily speedy. I start off missing an easy pass, giving the puck to the other team. They score a goal in the first three minutes. Boos ripple along the wall from all the home fans supporting us.

I heave a violent breath and steal a glance at Sophie. She's sitting on the edge of her seat, dialed in, wearing my slip up in the cringe on her face. It's been a long time since I had someone special watch me play.

Sure, my family catches the games when they're televised, but with the distance they rarely make it to an arena. They work, and I have bills. I promised myself that when I make it big in the NHL, I'm flying my parents out to every game. Until then having Sophie here fills a piece of that support I've been missing, fueling me to try harder.

It is only one missed pass.

I'll make it up.

Just as those thoughts cross my mind, the puck flies right by me, and the opposing defenseman snatches it up.

My jaw drops, and I crouch and speed up, racing to catch him. I lost my focus for a mere second but it's too late. The puck is en route, flying toward our goalie. I start pleading in my head.

Stop it!

Stop it!

Stop it!

And it's in!

Louder boos thicken the air, and I give the hardest eye roll ever. This can't be happening.

Two goals in five minutes.

It doesn't get any better. We are down three by intermission—all my fault—and I'm so mad I can hardly speak when we break. Coach Carlson's hardened gaze gives me a once over, but I bite back any harsh words. I only have myself to blame tonight. I didn't get here when I needed to, and my mind wasn't clear.

The second period is a true blood bath, as I vow to take the lead. I should be scoring goals, not giving them away. When I miss another shot again, the puck rattles around the boards and right into their possession. I muster every ounce of speed I have to catch him. I fly in front of him and start to skate backwards, jabbing at the puck with my stick. We continue to battle for the puck around the back end of our goal, and when I finally get my stick on the puck, it slides into the corner. As he skates over to resume control of the puck, I make a split decision and crosscheck him hard. There's no way he's taking another puck from me.

I already knew it was coming. The ref whistles the play dead, and I'm sent to the penalty box for two minutes.

Coach Carlson stands on the bench, arms crossed over his chest, his neutral expression fixed on me. When my time is up, I jump up, hungry to make up for my loss, but Coach calls me back to the bench.

I fight with every thread of dignity I have not to protest the call, and I skate over to take a seat on the bench.

For the *rest* of the game.

Hockey is always loud, but losses echo the heaviest.

When the final buzzer blares, my vision goes blurry, and the crowd's protests wind hauntedly around my head, and I feel dizzy.

Dissociating.

The team skates off the ice, and I remain in my spot warming the bench, letting all the losing sounds settle.

Hockey is a team sport.

But the failure is mine.

I hang my head, not moving for what feels like an eternity.

I don't even lift my head to say goodbye to Sophie.

The crowd thins.

Eventually they are all gone.

The TVs shut off.

The lights dim.

I hear a throat clear, and I lazily lift my eyes. Coach Carlson is standing next to me. I don't have it in me to make eye contact. He slaps a hand on my shoulder. "Got a sec?"

Ice slicks my veins, as I know he's going to come down hard on me.

This is where I'm normally a prick and run my mouth, but something's changed in me. Even though I feel this loss so deep in my gut I want to hurl, *I'm quiet.*

Bill steals my attention as he rounds the corner, saunters out of the tunnel, and joins us. "What do you have to say?" Bill asks, not unfriendly.

"I got nothing." I shrug exhaustively.

Bill lifts his hat, hovering it over his head while he scratches an itch on the top of his bald head with his other hand. "Something was different tonight. I've never seen you play like that."

"I was sloppy," I spit out, disgusted with myself. He doesn't have to assess my game as I already know I sucked.

"I think . . ." He pauses while he passes a look to Coach and goes after that itch on his head again. "I think I pushed you too hard. I got your mind off hockey, and now you're distracted by this whole fake-dating thing. The stunt with the jersey at the start of the game was too much. It made the crowd wild, and maybe that's what the problem was."

"That wasn't a stunt—"

He ignores my defenses. "We knew we couldn't keep this going forever, and the stands were packed, but that doesn't do us any good if we start losing all our games. Now, we need to reign things back. We can leak a statement that says you two parted ways as friends—"

"I'm not doing that." Fire pumps through my veins, and I burst to stand in front of Bill, looking down at him. "Nobody is going to release any statement about Sophie or me."

"It was fine at first," he tries to smooth things over, but rage is running through my brain. "It's taken a turn we weren't expecting. Having her at the game tonight was too much. We're going to streamline the distractions, and she's no longer allowed at the arena."

"You can't banish her from my games," I growl. "She's *my* girlfriend."

Bill wags his head, his eyelids getting heavy. "She's not your girlfriend. You forget this is all a setup." He starts to reach out to pat my shoulder, as if I need calming down, but I sweep his arm away. He doesn't understand that we've made a real connection and that everything's changed.

It's sort of funny, actually.

Our setup was all his idea, and I don't have anything to hide. He's the one person who knows the situation the best, and he'll surely laugh off the ending as good news. "Yes, I know it started that way, but things changed. We got to know each other for real, and we are officially together now."

"Axl." He goes after that itch again. I hold my breath, wondering if I should recommend some *Head & Shoulders*. After a painfully long pause, where I don't know what to say to convince him Sophie and I aren't faking it, he pulls out his phone and flicks open an app.

Then he hands me his phone.

Photo up.

My breath rushes fast, pumping adrenaline to every tendon in my body. "How did you get this photo?" I snatch the phone from him. "Are you spying on me?"

"I was." He nods matter-of-factly. "Look, after the reports came out that you two were faking it, I panicked. I knew this would not work unless we got you to loosen up in public. I don't know how to say this, but I knew you were the problem, being so stiff. I paid Sophie to kiss you. I thought if only she knew it was going to happen, it would look more natural, and I could leak the photo. We planned the whole thing, and I was waiting in the bushes to get proof."

"What?" I screech, my voice echoing off the walls. I suck in so much air, my nostrils flare. "You're lying."

"How would I have this photo if I was?" He shrugs, snatching his phone back and stuffing it into his pocket. "I'm no idiot. I see the way you look at her, and you're falling for her. Last night we took it too far. I'm sorry." He pats my shoulder. "I was hoping she'd say something, but it seems like she's keeping this charade going. I couldn't stand back and let your heart get broken . . . " His words drop off, and he turns to Coach. They exchange a quiet expression and walk away, leaving me to digest this.

I don't believe it.

But he has the proof on his phone.

This is absurd.

An agonizing laugh slips from my throat, even though I don't find a thing about this funny.

I'm a fool.

Nineteen

SOPHIE

I sit frozen in my seat, waiting for Axl to acknowledge me after the game, but it is clear he needs some time alone. I haven't seen this side of him before—the side where he's hard on himself. Guilt snakes back into my gut, reminding me that although the last two days have been magical, I can't ignore that Axl deserves to know the truth, even if it hurts him. If he's this hard on himself over one loss, I can't imagine how hard he'll be on me if he thinks I intentionally tricked him.

The thing is, we both went into this knowing it was fake, and we *both* had something to gain from the deception. He can't be mad at me for that part. I never expected the emotions to snowball, and I need to clear the air about this.

The timing is horrible.

He gave me his jersey!

I can't wear his jersey while knowing what I know.

The guilt is so thick that I'm nearly trembling, but I can't risk blurting anything out in public, so I race home. We need to talk tonight, but I struggle with what to say. I know he's down, and I decide to try to cheer him up. I text:

Sophie: I'm still wearing your jersey.

The dots immediately appear on my phone indicating he's texting back, and excitement bubbles in my gut.

Axl: Take it off!

Panic leaps in my throat, as the realization hits that something terrible has happened. I try to text, but my fingers are clumsy, and I'm afraid. Instead, I press call on his name and put the phone to my ear, and pray he picks up.

Who am I fooling?

Of course he doesn't answer, and hot tears prick the backs of my eyes. He's upset about the game, but he wouldn't say that to me unless something *else* happened.

And since there is something *terrible* he could find out, my mind goes to the worst.

He can't possibly know.

I cool my expression while I breathe and collect my purse and phone. I head down the hall, taking my mom's keys off the hook, and call to my parents, who are watching the news in the living room, "Going out. Taking the car."

"Where are you going?" Mom asks.

"I have to find Axl. I did something incredibly stupid, and I have to apologize." I wish I could lie, but I have a suspicion my lying days are over.

"Do you know where he lives?" Mom is crocheting something in her lap, but she manages to lift a brow in my direction while continuing her perfect stitches.

"I know the out-of-town players all stay in the apartments across from the rink."

"All except Axl," Mom says as she continues to stitch.

"How do you know that?"

"How do I know anything? Norma and her reliable church friends. She saw you last night sitting on the porch and came over earlier while you were gone. She made it a point to tell me everything she knows about him. For some reason that Norma couldn't figure out, even though she inquired about it to all her friends, Axl rents a room above the barber shop downtown. She says it's an older building, not even having air conditioning for the summer, and it's not nearly as nice as the new complex the other guys stayed at. She was wondering if I knew the scoop."

"Wow, thanks for the info, Mom." Normally, I'd chuckle at something so ridiculously nosey as this, but tonight, I want to thank my lucky church ladies. I slip my shoes on and call out, "Don't wait up for me!"

The weather has changed, and snow flurries flutter down. It's nothing threatening but it makes driving at night a little hard, especially once I get into town and have to deal with the glaring light from the lamp posts. I know exactly where the barber shop is, and I don't slow down until I'm parked outside of it. Sure enough, Axl's truck is parked in the alley.

I kill the engine, nearly tumbling out of the car, but something catches me.

Movement in my peripheral vision.

There's a little park in the center of the town square. It's where they set up the Christmas tree after Thanksgiving, and they do flea markets here in the summer. There's also a little manmade wishing pond that's purposely frozen into a skating rink in the winter

Someone's on it.

I don't need to ask Norma and her reliable church friends why Axl would live here.

This pond closely resembles the one he described from back home.

And if he's still feeling down on himself, it makes sense that this is where he'd be.

It's chilly, but I barely notice as I'm still scared. I jog across the street, and I know he can see me as I'm the only other moving thing out here at this time of night, but he doesn't turn my way. He's slamming the puck into the cement wall that surrounds the rink, rebounding it, and repeating.

Ignoring me.

My steps falter when they meet the edge of the rink. "Axl."

"I told you to take that jersey off," he growls, still not meeting my gaze as he fires off another puck at the back wall.

I suddenly know what happened.

There's nothing else that makes sense. "Bill talked to you."

His eyes slam to mine, and he rasps, "So you admit it?"

"I-I . . . Yes, uh, yeah." I'm not making excuses. He deserves the truth, and I take a deep breath and let everything rush out. "I thought it was a terrible idea, but he insisted it would make everything better and help us both. I didn't think you liked me, or that it would matter, and we both already agreed to fake this. My tour is running out of money, and my crew hasn't even been fully compensated yet. He offered to pay their salaries, and I caved. That was before, though."

"It was yesterday." He scowls. "You can't tell me you changed your mind since yesterday."

"I can't explain it." I lift my shaking shoulders, willing to let all my honesty out. "You said it best when you said that the kiss changes it all. For me, it did."

"What did it change?" His eyes snap up, and his expression can only be described as cold.

I shake my head. It's so silly considering it's only been a day, but everything feels different. "I went from feeling like we had a job to do . . . to I don't know." I wag my head, giving up. I have messed everything up. "I'm so sorry, Axl," I squeak out. "I never meant to hurt you, but I wasn't faking it anymore."

His lips twist into a cocky snarl. "So, tell me, how much does a kiss from me cost?"

My jaw drops, and I can't spit out a rebuttal fast enough. "I didn't take any money, and I won't!"

"You didn't take any money," he says coldly, his eyes narrowing on me, "because you haven't had time to cash the check?"

"No," I assert, knowing I'll never convince him. It's hopeless. I did this to myself. I should have known better. This whole thing started as a way to get revenge on Rocco, and my getting my heart broken *again* is likely karma for my ill intentions. I reach down, taking the hem of Axl's jersey in my hand, and pull it over my head.

I'm still wearing my pink sweatshirt, and even though I loved it this morning, I hate it now because it's not Axl's jersey. "I don't know how else to tell you I'm sorry," I choke out. When he doesn't move to take the jersey, I fold it neatly into a square. With trembling fingers, I lay it on the ground next to the rink.

He still doesn't budge.

In my head, I beg him to say he understands. I turn on my heel, ready to trudge back to the car, when he calls out. "Is there any other lie you need to confess?"

I spin on my heel, panicking that he believes something else, and I shout, "No, there's nothing else! The only other lies are the ones you are in on, but I know I'll never lie again. It's exhausting, and I feel so terrible."

"I have one." His stony glare smacks me hard.

"One w-what?" I stutter, but answer myself, "You have a lie?"

He slips one foot in front of the other, slowly sliding my way, but his expression softens, and at least for right now, I gather his temper has cooled. When he glides to a perfect stop on the edge of the ice, squaring his body with mine, I hold my breath. He doesn't mince words. "I knew something was off last night. Don't get me wrong, I wanted to kiss you, but I could tell you weren't completely comfortable. Your timing was terrible. And everything was rushed."

"You knew! Then why did you kiss me?" I blurt. "Why did you say all that about how it changes everything? Because I believed it!"

"I thought you were just being silly." He threw his hand up, cutting me off. "And that's why I warned you. I was confused about how you made that leap. I thought you were bluffing or something, but when you accepted my terms, that's when everything changed. Everything changed *before* the kiss. You stopped being uncomfortable and goofy, and we connected. I just can't believe you'd play me like that, because you ruined something that could have been amazing by destroying my trust before we even had a chance to try."

"I destroyed your trust," I echo, my voice losing strength as my worst nightmare is coming true.

He pulls one side of his lips up in a cocky grin as he spins on his heel, skating farther from me. "I'm curious how much a kiss from me goes for."

"I would never put a dollar amount on it," I say, my tear-stained words following him. "I'm so sorry, Axl," I cry out. "I never meant to hurt you, but I also never expected these emotions to be so strong, and I promise I'm not faking it anymore. Will you forgive me?"

"No." His single word echoes into the night air.

Panic pounds through my chest, engulfing my heart, but he's skating far away without even sneaking a look back. In an odd way, I understand his betrayal, because I lived betrayal with Rocco. I just never thought I'd be capable of causing this. I fight to maintain my composure. This is nobody's fault but my own. "I understand," I reply softly, but deep down, I can't ignore the aching in my chest. For the tiniest glimmer of a moment, I fooled myself into believing that I would be happy this time.

With my heart in my throat, I sulk back to my mom's car, but I can't shake the dejection that clings to my heart like a steel cloak. Once again, I'm returning home to Mama with a broken heart.

Twenty

Sophie

Unable to sleep, I roll out of bed early and curl up onto my papasan chair like I did when I was a teenager. It's a good thinking chair. As I scan my poster-clad wall, I don't find anything to provide comfort. Too bad I didn't have a little lapdog or something to keep me company while I'm feeling down and lonely.

Loneliness is new to me.

I'm usually too busy for loneliness. If I'm honest, I'd say I'm also feeling shame over how I misused Axl's trust. I can't even cry about feeling hurt, because it really is all my fault for being so stupid to think it was okay to trick him. As I replay the moment when he gave me his jersey, I remember how his whole face was lit up in adoration.

Neither one of us was acting.

The thing is, I didn't know we'd catch those kinds of feelings for each other after just one kiss. We'd been hanging out for days, and although the attraction was there, we'd been able to keep everything professional. Then he flipped some sort of switch where, as soon as we crossed that boundary, he treated me as his princess, and I believed it. I'm so dumb. I smash my palm on my forehead, wishing for a do-over just as my phone vibrates. I don't need to check before I answer. "Morning, Bails," I sing out gloomily.

"Man, do you sound terrible," she teases. "Were you out all night celebrating with your boyfriend?"

"No." I'm monotone, not trying to hide my sorrow. I might as well end the charade now, as Axl's not going to want to hang out with me anymore. "I think we broke up."

"Oh, Soph, honey, I'm so sorry. What happened?"

"Nothing really happened." I start to recite the lines we'd rehearsed about our breakup since day one of this thing. "We had so much fun together, and it was a bit of a whirlwind, but we decided neither one of us is ready for a relationship. I wish the best for *him*." My voice squeaks as I roll my bottom lip in. I don't know why this sucks so bad. I knew it wasn't real from the beginning.

"Oh, girl, you say it's nothing, but you sound so heartbroken. I'm so sorry."

I bite harder on my lip, unable to squeak out an argument. Tears prick my eyes, and I fight the urge to cry out about what a loser I am to have messed this up so badly. I know better than to deceive people like that. I deserve every ounce of heartbreak I get.

"I suppose this is a good time to tell you that I have fantastic news."

"You do?" I sniff and slightly perk up.

"I got a check from Bill. He said it was for some marketing campaign you've been helping the team with. I have no idea what you're doing, but boy is he generous. It's amazing, and it's enough to cover everyone's bonuses and more."

A knot bubbles in my throat. That's not good news! Bill isn't supposed to pay me. I can't spend that money. Now, I'll have to come up with some excuse about why I need to give it back, and the lies will never end. This is the exact opposite of good news.

"Are you still there?" Bailey peeps out in a softer voice.

"I am. Maybe I'm a little more overwhelmed than I thought I was about everything."

"I bet. You've had a crazy couple of weeks. I don't suppose you heard about Rocco?"

My brain slams into what feels like another realm. I haven't even thought about him, and it feels weird to hear his name. "What girl is he on the beach with this week?" I honestly couldn't care less about him at this point.

"No beaches. Looks like you weren't the only one he was cheating on. He just got outed in the NFL for some cheating scandal."

"What do you mean?" My brow furrows. "How can he cheat in the NFL?"

"I guess he was taking bets or something, and purposely missing plays. It's a whole thing they uncovered between him and a few of his teammates. He's out of the league as of last night."

"I didn't hear that." I shake my head back and forth, feeling numb. Maybe our breakup was a blessing, because now I'm no longer tied to him. Nobody can drag me through his scandal.

"That sounds awful, but I guess I'm not surprised. He tends to think he's above the rules."

"Yeah, it's a mess."

My mind is reeling. It has only been a couple of days since I talked to Bailey, and this morning she's full of information. "Is that everything?"

"Almost." Her tone takes a higher pitch as if she's getting ready to pry.

"What now?" My heart ticks up. "Please tell me you saved the best news for last."

"I'm getting asked to schedule interviews, and a few radio shows are requesting you. I've been putting everyone off, but I'd like a date for when you're coming back to work."

I let out a sigh that borders on a huff. I love my job. I'm grateful to do what I do. She's also right. I need to put my big-girl pants on and schedule a date. With my fake-date gig over, there's no need for me to hang out in Mapleton anymore. "Give me the weekend. I'll fly back on Monday morning. If you need to schedule anything, I'll be ready that evening." My heart constricts. Something about leaving Mapleton feels so final. I feel like if I don't get this thing with Axl resolved, it'll never get fixed, and I prefer to at least part amicably.

"Sounds good. Oh, and if you're bored," she rushes out. "you are certainly welcome to work on some new music."

"What?" My head literally jolts back as if she's hitting me with the most shocking news ever.

"You write the best songs when you're heartbroken."

"I'm not heart—" I cut myself off. She's right. That's what I am. Bailey knows me best. I've never been one to talk too much about my problems. I prefer to funnel everything into my creative outlet, which is one of the reasons I came here after Rocco cheated on me. I wanted some time to relax and have my music therapy, but I got so wrapped up in this fake-dating thing, it never happened. "Maybe I will." I'm thoughtful as I say goodbye. I stare at my phone for only a moment before I open a note in it and start playing with words.

"Mama." I crack open my bedroom door, hollering down the hall. "Come upstairs. I want to show you something."

"Is it more photos of you?" Her voice gets louder, and a hint of laughter trickles out as she teases, "I might need a warning."

"No more photos." I wave her forward and quickly shut my door before Sam catches wind of what I'm doing. I love my brother, but I don't doubt for a second that he'll betray me and find some way to contact Axl before I'm ready.

Mama has her salt and pepper curls pinned back out of her face with two bobby pins, the way she wears it when she's ready for church. "It's not Sunday." I stare at her hair, wondering if I got my days mixed up.

"Oh, this." Patting her hair, Mama smiles slyly. "I'm getting together with Norma and the church ladies for tea, so I put myself together."

"Please don't let her talk about me again." I exhaustibly huff, tilting my head toward her. "She needs to get a life."

"You know me." Mama's brows rise in unison. "I'm a good listener, and I've learned that my listening skills can be mighty useful." Her eyes twinkle as they stare into mine.

"*What* do you know?" My tone is extra sharp, as all the possible stories buzz through my mind, and I whine, "Why is she so concerned about me?"

"Not you," Mama nearly whispers as she gushes. "She heard that some high-fluting NHL coach is in town, looking for talented players, and it seems like Axl's on the top of his list."

My stomach churns as I recall Axl's part of our pact. He's getting exactly what he wants, and I should be happy for him. Part of me is happy for him, but the other part already misses him. Once he gets signed, he'll leave Mapleton. Since he has no ties here, there'll be no reason to ever come back. "He's been working really hard, and that's amazing news for him." I lower my voice, concealing my emotions. "He never accepted my apology."

Mama's green eyes darken as she takes another step into the room. "I'm sorry. Is there something I can help with?"

"I was working on a new song for him but look what I found." My gaze drifts to my guitar, which I propped up against my papasan chair. It's acoustic and the first guitar I ever received. I was only ten when Mama got it for me. It's burned into all my memories, and for that reason alone I could never get rid of it, despite the many upgrades I've had.

"Oh, yes, that old thing. I knew it was up here. Does it even tune anymore?"

"It does." My fingers trace the strings. This guitar changed my life for two reasons. One, it was the moment music was brought into my life. And two, it taught me a valuable lesson, because it wasn't just the gift that was memorable, but the way Mama gave it to me. It had been the first Christmas after Sam was born, and I was having a hard adjustment. Being a big sister wasn't at all what I thought it was going to be because Sam was colicky and screamed all day, leaving no time for Mama and me to hang out. Not to mention, I had no presents under the tree. I wasn't overly upset because I trusted Mama hadn't forgotten about me, and I figured she was up to something. When it came time to open gifts, she gave me the end of a string and smiled. Lost at first, I was even a little offended, but eventually I took the hint and walked with the string. It led me all around the house on a scavenger hunt until it finally took me to the front porch where she had a box. Inside the box was the guitar. More than getting a gift, I was left with the feeling of being so loved because of all the time and thought Mama put into it. It was all the feelings I needed to make up for the weeks of feeling passed over for the new baby.

Mama taught me the lesson that the presentation can make someone feel more special than the actual gift. That's the mantra I've followed in my career, and it's what made me connect easier with fans. I've tried to carry that into all my shows and songs.

It's not just about a brand, it's about an experience, and I want everyone to feel like they are part of it.

Hmm.

My mind automatically shifts back to Axl. He was blindsided by the news of my deception, which was not a good way to break it to him at all, and then I practically ambushed him at the park when he clearly wanted to be left alone. I could have handled that so much better.

Maybe if I put some thought into it . . . another shot at apologizing could work? "You know something?" I look up at my mom while grabbing my guitar by the neck and sitting on the chair, positioning myself to play. "I was working on a new song, trying to funnel some of my disappointment into something productive, but what do you think about the idea of me playing it for *Axl* when it's done?"

Her expression softens and she reaches out, touching my forearm, and gives it a soft squeeze. "I think it's worth a shot." Mama's proud smile beams as she slowly backs out of the door. "I need to run or I'll be late, but I can't wait to hear it when I get back."

"Love you." I keep my eyes on my guitar as I adjust the strings, and a tiny seed of hope fills my chest. An apology will work, but I just need to do it with a little *presentation.*

Twenty-One

Axl

The crowd becomes unglued, screaming out explosive cheers as the puck flies past the goalie and into the net seconds before the period ends. I raise my arms in triumph, a victorious grin spreading across my face as the buzzer sounds. When the second period is over, momentum has shifted in Granite Ice's favor. It's the best possible thing that could happen. Coach has his NHL friend, Mike Stevens, in the owner's box today, and he's been glued to my every move.

My stomach has been a fireball of nerves all day, and I can't believe after all the years of hard work and sacrifice, my dreams might finally come true. Sure, I had a little help from Sophie and that ridiculous stunt we pulled, but the NHL isn't here to look at my social media photos. They are here to watch me play.

Sweat beads down my brow, and I swipe it away just as Noah raises his glove to give me knuckies, and together we skate off the ice for intermission. Usually, the music is on by now, pumping the team and crowd back up. It's oddly quiet until the chords of an acoustic guitar cut into the intercom system. It's so out of place that it pricks my ears. Sometimes the team managers allow a special spotlight on a local charity cause, and I cut a glance to the overhead screens, immediately wishing I hadn't.

Cold sweat slides down my back.

I'm in a nightmare.

My blood runs frigid through my veins, and my heart ramps up at turbo speeds. This can't be happening. I slowly scan the crowd, praying it's my imagination playing tricks on me, but all the fans are glued to the screen, too.

Full center on the screen, Sophie stands on the ice and in front of the camera with a junkie guitar strapped around her shoulders, and she's strumming away like we're about to impart on some parade. My throat dries and I wish I could scream out, but that would only draw more attention to whatever stunt she's playing. I pinch my arm, praying I wake up from this nightmare, but nothing happens. This is no nightmare—this is real.

Just when I think it can't possibly get any worse, she opens her mouth and begins to sing. She has a lovely voice, but it doesn't take a genius to see what's happening when she belts out the first phrase.

I know my apology won't take back
The fact that I hurt you.
But please know I'm sorry
With every word in this song

This is the most embarrassing thing that has ever happened to me. I raise my glove over my brow and cringe as heat floods to my face. Is she seriously up there making a fool of herself to apologize? Did she purposely not make it rhyme? She has to know this song is terrible.

With the NHL coach watching me, this is the biggest night of my career.

This can't be happening.

I shoot daggers out of my eyes, running my hand over my throat, signaling her to cut out, but she just keeps singing.

I'm sorry for my selfishness
I'm sorry I hurt you
But it was never my intention

The overhead screen splits, and now one side shows me, and I'm dying. The whole crowd knows the song is about me, and my face fires hotter than an oven. I have to take matters into my own hands, and I skate toward her, and everyone in the crowd holds their collective breath. You can hear every slice of my skate, and I'm at a loss at what to do. She's completely lost her mind, but if I'm a prick and run my mouth—the way I usually do—I'm surely going to get kicked off the team. My reputation will also be ruined, because I guarantee every starry-eyed female in this room right now is rooting for us to get back together.

It can't happen.

But Sophie will not stop singing!

I thought I was strong, but now I'm trembling,
My heart is quaking inside my chest.

I fight to hold on but it's all quicksand.

"Sophie," I growl. "Stop it. You're making a fool out of your-self."

She just keeps singing, *"Maybe that's what this kiss was meant to do?"*

"Sophie, this isn't helping anything." She clearly can't see how ridiculous this looks. Unless she does see . . . but doesn't care.

Maybe that's the point?

Maybe she's purposely embarrassing herself to make a point. My brows lower, and I tune into her not-melodic lyrics.

Force us both to change.

Do you need some more apologies?

I'm sorry I made you feel less than the amazing person you are

But most of all, I'm sorry for not kissing you more when I had the chance, because I really like kissing yooooou.

The women in the crowd start to chant, "Kiss her," and I'm frozen. Sophie keeps singing these terrible lyrics and putting her-self out there in the most public way, and she wouldn't be doing this if she didn't want to. If it didn't mean something to her.

All I can do is apologize and hope that one day you'll forgive me.

So, kiss me again.

I can make up verses all night. It's in your best interest to kiss me now.

It's only going to get worse.

She's right about her song getting worse!

She's not even singing on key. It's as if she wants to humble herself, but as ridiculous as this is, she looks beautiful. Her hair is long and straight and falls in front of one shoulder as she leans over and strums her guitar.

My gaze slides to the owner's box, and Bill and Mike are getting a front-row seat to all of this.

Figures.

It's hopeless.

I'm sure she's already destroyed any chances of me getting signed by now.

The crowd chants louder, "Kiss her," and I'm doomed.

At this point, kissing her seems to be the only way she'll ever stop singing.

If I hadn't lived through these last couple of weeks, I wouldn't believe any of the events could even be possible—that I could fall for someone from just one kiss.

And here she is, fighting for another chance and willing to risk total humiliation. I'm not a monster. She's only human.

And just like that, I melt.

All the tense energy falls from my head and is replaced with a pooling in my heart. Tears prick the back of my eyes, and I can't believe how close I came to screwing this up and missing it completely. Before I talk myself out of it—and before Sophie can make up an even worse verse—I skate to the exit and walk to meet her.

Her hand freezes mid-strum, and her gorgeous green eyes hover on mine. "Can we just start over?" Her plea tumbles out, and she's not even trying to be discreet.

"We can't start over." My rasp is quick and assertive, and I don't wait for permission as I lean in and wrap my arms around her waist, digging my fingers lightly into the small of her back. "Remember. I meant what I said. The whole thing has changed, and there's no going back."

Her breath audibly hitches, like she's holding back a hiccup. I raise my hand, cupping her cheek. Her eyelids lower, hooding her eyes, and I curl my toes in anticipation. My fingers sprawl out to tickle just below her ear, and I tip her chin up until our lips brush together, and we both *confirm* everything has changed.

And the crowd goes wild.

Oh yeah, we do come back for the third period and win our game. I was offered a contract, but after consulting my heart, I decided it wasn't the best fit for me right now. I want to stay in Mapleton for another year. This little town and their Granite Ice team have taken my heart by storm. Not to mention, Sophie played a bit of a role in it.

Epilogue

Six Months Later

Tap, tap.

I don't move to open the door. Axl knows he's always welcome. It's my first week in my new apartment in Mapleton. I'd been commuting back and forth to see Axl, but after my last tour concluded, I decided to take some time off to write some new music. I set up a small recording studio in the extra bedroom in this apartment. Axl's not musical at all, but he's been coming over every day after morning hockey practice to listen to me do my thing.

The door flies open, and Axl's carrying my coffee order—that I didn't order—as he's assumed the princess treatment my driver used to give me. He leans over and drops a sweet, chaste kiss on my lips before blurting out, "Morning, Twinkie." The rascal smile on his face is instant.

I jolt to stand and search for a pillow or something nearby to hurl at him. When I don't find anything I can't risk breaking, I settle with a warning. "You're not allowed to talk to Sam anymore."

He sets my coffee on top of my desk and takes the empty seat in front of my keyboard. His finger instantly finds the keys in front of him, and he plucks away without any rhythm.

"Sounds great, babe," I tease in between swallowing drinks of my hot coffee.

"I've been practicing, and I'm thinking of making a career change." He bombs out a disorganized chord. "What do you think? Would you hire me as a keyboard player?"

"Only for your looks."

"Oh, I see how you are." He runs his fingers all along the keys, and not one chord sounds good. When he throws in a very off-key *do re mi*, I struggle not to cringe. But he's laughing, clearly joking around. "So, no backup singing gig during my off season?" He wags his brows at me.

"I mean . . . you just hit every note on every scale that ever existed so clearly this is your future." Laughter rushes out from both of our mouths, and he spins on the chair to face me.

"I'm so glad you see it my way, because I decided that now that this last tour of yours is over, I don't want to go back to only seeing you a couple times a month. I'm happy to moonlight as a backup singer."

"I'll jot that down in my notes in case I ever lose my hearing." I cross the room and plop down on his lap, wrapping one arm around his neck.

His tongue juts out, and he pretends to struggle to breathe under my weight. "What's wrong with your chair?"

"Nothing. I just like this one better." I giggle, enjoying all the ways we are never serious together. I swap my expression to a serious one. "I'm glad you brought that up."

"Brought what up? How nice your chair is?"

"Not my chair." I playfully punch his shoulder. "About my tour being over and not wanting to spend time apart, because I decided that it's time for me to take a vacation. I booked a month-long trip traveling all over Europe, but I don't want to go by myself. Would you know anybody who wants to go?"

"There's no way I could possibly be your chair for a month," he huffs out, and I lose it, nearly falling to the ground with laughter.

"Stop it and be serious." I stand, being stubborn. "Happy now?"

Without wasting a second, he stands too, pulling me into him. One of his hands slides around my back and the other cups my cheek. "No, I'm not happy yet."

My lips part, but he slides his hand over and presses a finger to my lips, silencing me.

"Now that we're living in the same town, I think we need to set some rules."

"About not sitting on your lap?" I struggle not to laugh because his finger is still glued to my lips.

"Well, yes, and about everything else. Things are different for us—"

"I call we get to kiss!" I cut in, still giggling.

"Oh, yes," he asserts. "There'll be lots of kissing, but I'm think-ing about some things, and there's something I need you to know. Three things actually, because I play hockey and I'm always going for the hat trick."

"Okaaay."

"First." He finally removes his finger from my lips only to hold it up in front of my face like I don't understand what the number one is, making me giggle. "I'm going to let you down."

My brows furrow, and my heart plummets. That is not what I expect. My thoughts run on a loop, trying to figure out what he'd done wrong.

"Not every day," he continues, "but that's life, and it's going to happen."

The pit of my stomach feels as if it's about to flip upside down. I have no idea where this is coming from. *What did he do?*

"That leads me to number two." He tacks up another finger. I'm not even close to laughing now. *I'm afraid.* "I won't give up. I'll do the work, not because I'm desperate, but because we're worth it."

Relief floods my veins when I realize something terrible hasn't happened. He's saying something incredibly sweet, which makes tears prick the backs of my eyes.

"Number three." His voice is softer, and languid, pulling on all my heartstrings. "I'll protect you. That doesn't need any other explanation. And finally . . . because I'm an overachiever, there needs to be an extra point." I'm quiet, but his hand finds my cheek again and he drops his face so close to mine I feel the warmth of his skin over mine. His eyes hood, and I assume number four is a kiss, so I close my eyes and lean in.

Instead of finding his lips, I hear his words hot on my skin. "I'll love you. Not flawlessly as I'm not without my faults, but I'll give you my everything."

My upper lip is literally sweating.

We've never used the *L word* before. I've wanted to, but I waited for him, and now that he finally slips it out, I'm dying.

"I love you, too." I don't have a speech like that. I've never heard anything so beautiful in my life, and my lips nearly quiver. I can't handle being this close to him for another second. "Can you just kiss me already?"

"Pucker up."

And I did.

BONUS EPILOGUE

Some time later . . .

"Let's stop here," I huff out right as we round another bend in our trail. We're staying at a mountain cabin in the Alps, trying to make progress on Axl's goal of *hiking all the trails*. I don't mind hiking, but I'm rethinking our strategy for his bucket list. "I think next time we start with swimming in all the oceans first." I brace my hands above my knees and continue with my deep breathing.

His chuckle is airy. "Sorry, I forget that not everyone trains four to six hours a day."

"Nope, I sure don't do that." I debate stretching my hands over my head to try to loosen my back, but I'm wholeheartedly concerned I might get stuck. I settle on rubbing my side ache.

"It's a good thing I came prepared." Axl drops his backpack to the ground, and my gaze follows his every move as my interest piques. He pulls out something that looks like a ball of fabric, and his lips pinch in secret as he unrolls the ball.

"A hammock," I exclaim, already moving my legs toward it as it sounds wonderful. "I knew there was a reason I love you so much." I arch my neck, pretending to peek in his bag. "Now, do you have any dark chocolate in that thing?"

"No, sorry. I opted for healthier trail mix to keep up our energy." He walks to a tree and leans on it, testing it for safety. He must have been pleased with what he discovered because he gets busy hanging the hammock, and within minutes, it's ready for business. He holds his hand out, inviting me over. "Try it."

"Is that a dare?" He doesn't have to ask me twice. I drop my backpack and ease myself down onto the hammock. My whole body seems to contract from the release of pressure, and I sigh in contentment. "It's amazing. Hop in."

Axl follows my lead, carefully balancing the hammock with me in it, as he adds his weight. With one of his hands behind his head and the other under me, we fit together quite perfectly.

A stillness comes over us, and we take in the view while the hammock sways gently in the breeze. The sun is beginning its descent, casting a warm golden glow over the valley. I close my eyes to the sound of the wind playing with the leaves, feeling completely at peace. "This is what I'm talking about," I tease with my eyes still closed as I try to soak up the last of the summer rays before they disappear for the night.

"We should maybe change our goals to sleep in all the trees instead of hiking all the trails." Axl's voice moves close to my ear before he drops a kiss on my cheek.

"Yes, we should. Jot that down."

"Hey." Axl's voice grows softer. "Do you want to open your eyes for a minute before you fall asleep?"

"Want to?" I tease, still keeping them shut. "No. But will I?" I pull one eye open, ready to compromise, but then instantly follow with the other eye all the while my breath gets locked in my chest. I look at Axl—the love of my life—who is holding out a beautiful princess-cut diamond ring. Tears well in my eyes as I have dreamed of this moment so many times, and I sit up. "What is that?"

"Let me do this properly." Axl's voice fills with sincerity as he slides off the hammock and drops down on one knee. When his eyes lock on me, we sync like the last piece of a thousand-piece puzzle is finally getting clicked into place. "I made you three promises, and what you didn't know at the time was in my heart I already knew you were the one. I want to add one more promise to that list. I promise if you marry me, I will spend the rest of my life putting you first." For a fleeting moment, even the wind stills, and I gaze into his eyes as his lips appear to move in slow motion. "Will you marry me?"

I don't need to think, but I want to savor the moment. I pause, burning the image into my brain. "Yes, I will." His usually strong hand—that was trained to perfectly steady a hockey stick—visibly trembles when he slips the ring on my finger. It fits perfectly.

Just as I drop my gaze to admire the ring, a rustling in the bushes nearby makes my heart skip a beat. We both frantically scan the trees for any sign of movement. All I see is a row of berry bushes, but that's not the best sign because berries can be food for a lot of big animals—including bears. I can't make anything out, but panicked inflections take over my voice. "Please say that's a wild monkey."

Axl slowly rises to his feet. "Sophie, we might need to leave."

I ease off the hammock and reach for the keychain I have clipped to my belt loop with bear spray. "Next time you propose, can you check for bears first?" I whisper teasingly as we slowly back away from the hammock and grab our backpacks with minimal movement.

"I think we stick to the beach next time." He raises a hand on the small of my back and guides me to the trail.

"Maybe your promise should have been how you weren't going to let me get eaten by bears." I struggle to hold a straight face.

"Oh, Soph." He sighs, holding back a chuckle, but he pulls me even closer to him as we descend the trail together, putting distance between the bush and us. "You seem to forget the last time we got interrupted by a bush." I raise a brow in silence, as he tacks on, "It turned out pretty well."

"That it did." I nod and link arms with Axl as we set back off on the trail, not quite sure where it is taking us, but I'm content to know we'll always have each other, even if we have to buy a new hammock.

"Okay." I sigh, as we are far enough away from the bush that I can't see it anymore. "Can we stop for a moment?"

Axl halts fast, turning toward me. "Are you feeling all right?"

"Yeah, it's nothing like that." I wave dismissively. "I was thinking. Now that we're engaged, we need to set some ground rules."

"Is that so?" One corner of his lips curls into a mischievous smirk.

"It is so, and it's not really a rule as much as it's a pact," I say, waiting to see the recognition flicker in his eyes. "The pact is to never go to bed, do anything, or go anywhere without kissing first, appropriately named the kiss-all-the-time, as-much-as-possible pact."

His eyes sparkle all the hues of blue down on me, and he lowers his chin, stopping right before our lips meet. "Deal. Should we kiss on it?"

"We shall." I nod and close my eyes, waiting for the pact to begin.

Dear Reader – Guess what? Rocco started as a villain in another book. I enjoyed writing him so much, I reused him for The Puck-er Up Pact. If you'd like to peek at his other cameo, please enjoy the following excerpt from No More Mr. Chai Guy, which is coming to Kindles September 12th, 2024, and already available for preorder.

North Newson

"I'm open!" My throat burns with hot breath as I emit a scream that formed from the bottom of my gut. I weave to dodge defensive player #22. Our star running back, Rocco Bella, hurls a long pass at me. I lunge forward, grappling for the football, barely staying upright, if not for the tips of my toes. Once I regain my footing, I'm gone.

Destination: endzone.

"Ladies and gentlemen," the announcer's voice ticks up in tension, running back #47, North Newson, has the ball, and he's heading to the endzone!" The crowd rushes to their feet with fanatical screaming. I pump my legs faster while the announcer echoes over the speakers. "Forty yards, he's going for it!"

I'm lightning, but my immediate goal is to be even faster. I dig in and pull as much speed as I can. This touchdown is all we need to take the lead, and we are down to two minutes on the clock. I don't even want to think about the scout in the stands tonight who made it clear he was watching both Rocco and me. It's both of our goals to play in the NFL, and winning this game could make both our dreams come true. "Thirty yards!"□ the announcer counts down, his voice on edge. The crowd becomes unhinged.

A linebacker's behind me now. He's so close, his breath puffs out in audible waves, which make the hairs on the back of my neck stand up. My chest drums out explosions, as my heart crawls into my throat and I top out my speed. I'm almost there. Twenty more yards.□

Cramps snake up my calves, begging me to slow down, but my mind is a tank, and I refuse to cave to any pain.

The linebacker finds a burst of speed, rushing my side, but I'm slick and weave to the side, dodging him. The crowd rumbles with so much noise, it's as if the bleachers are about to collapse, and the ground is going to split open. The linebacker isn't done, and he is back on my side again. There's nowhere for me to go! I'm blazing forward and being run out of bounds.

There's someone here!

A cheerleader in mid-cheer.

I frantically swipe my hand to push her out of the way, but she's not paying attention and *wham*! We collide. I tumble over her, taking her with me, and we roll together off the field all the while the crowd is roaring.

When we finally stop turning, I steal my gaze forward. I'm laying smack on top of Gia Bella.

Head cheerleader.

Prettiest girl in school.

Rocco's little sister.

She also just happens to be the woman I've been secretly in love with for *years*.

Her gaze hooks mine, and our breaths heave out, blending as we freeze together by instant magnetism.

"North! Nice job throwing the game for us," Rocco sarcastically screams as he jogs to the sidelines, anger oozing out of his eyes. "And get off my sister!"

Ice pumps through my veins as my body awakens to the fact that
I'm lying on top of Gia Bella! I quickly roll off her, face fiery with
embarrassment, and I pray we can laugh this whole thing off. As I
rush to my feet, I reach back to offer Gia a hand up, but her face
pinches and she grabs her knee.

The crowd quickly hushes, and it's so quiet you can hear a fly
fart. "Are you okay?" I whisper as if the sound will cause her more
pain.

Her silky ponytail cascades over her shoulder, shielding her face
from me, but it doesn't fully conceal her clenching eyes with a
single tear drop below the left one.

I suck in a hard breath.

She's hurt.

I did this to her.

I blink, and Rocco slides in next to her, pushing me to fade to
the background before I have a chance to plead sorry. She's quickly
surrounded by medics. Her dad flies out of the bleachers, huddling
in, and then she's whisked off the field. My team's lining up again,
but I'm frozen.

"North!" Coach yells at me. "You're benched."

Of course, I am!

At this point I hardly care about the game, as my heart's slamming against my ribcage, panting Gia's name. I want to run after
her, but there's nothing I can do for her.

The game must go on.

I regretfully take my seat on the edge of the bench, while my teammates pound my back. "Wrong kind of touchdown, Bruh," someone snickers.

Rocco returns, glaring at me through narrowed eyes, smeared with his eye black, and he grumbles, "You know, you just ruined everything. We were supposed to win tonight."

"How is she?" I rise to my feet, searching his face for clues.

"Stay away from my sister," he growls while piercing his eyes into mine, sending a chill spiraling through them all the way down to my toes.

"It was clearly an accident," My voice is resolute, and I take a solid step back from Rocco. A switch has been flipped, and Rocco's grin widens as he steps closer, closing the gap I had just created, while invading my personal space.

"You better watch your back," he sneers, his breath hot on my face. But as he raises his fist to strike, coach comes out from behind us, freezing us both in place.

"To the bench, boys. *Now!*"

She's fine, I reassure myself, as I pivot, and plop down on the bench, hanging my head. I've taken way worse hits than that and walked them off. She'll be right back out in a few moments. I stare down the path that leads to the locker rooms, waiting.

Please come out and be okay.

But she never returns to the field.

Acknowledgements

I'm always amazed how God continues to put the right people in my life at the exact moment I can use some help. For this book, I reconnected with an editor who I worked with years ago. I had no idea at the time I reached out to him but soon found out that he used to play hockey and is an *expert*.

What luck!

Well, I know it isn't luck as much as it is how God takes care of things for me. So, special thanks to Darcy for all the help with the hockey sequences, and my entire team of editors.

Also, special thanks to fellow sweet hockey author, Kerry Evelyn, for your encouragement with this series and friendship.

And as always, thank you to my amazing readers and this whole book community. It's an honor to have my little space in the book world.

Of course, my husband and kids. They put up with me writing these books all the time as I chase my dreams.

Last but not because he's least. My writing partner who has slugged through all my books with me. You know who you are.

About J.P. Sterling

J.P. Sterling grew up watching old reruns of Lucille Ball and Mary Tyler Moore and fell in love with wholesome entertainment and slapstick comedy. She loves leaning into the over-the-top humor and full circle moments, especially if it means the underdog gets to shine.

Aside from writing, she's also a wife and homeschooling mom, a holistic dietitian, a former college professor and lover of all-things dark chocolate.

*No swears. Just kisses. No Blasphemies. *

Let's get social!

Hey you amazing reader! You are invited to join my private reader group for all-things clean books and friends. Enter the group here: https://www.facebook.com/groups/1500850764081965

Other places to follow me:

Instagram: https://www.instagram.com/stories/authorjpsterling/

Facebook: https://www.facebook.com/jpsterlingauthor/

Amazon: https://www.amazon.com/stores/author/B01N9TJXJN/about

Also by J.P. Sterling

Bosses and Billionaires Series (**All Standalones**)

Maid for my Billionaire Boss

Upcycling My Rig-Pig Boss

Kissed by My Billionaire Boss

Marooned with My Celebrity Boss

***Christmas Shenanigans* (All Standalones)**

Mingle All the Way

Tis the Season to Get Married

***The Coffee Loft Series (*All Standalones)**

Pardon My French Press

No More Mr. Chia Guy (Coming Fall 2024)

***A Modern Fairy Tale Series (*All Standalones)**

Royally Rugged

Royally Guarded (Coming Fall 2025)

A Heart that Dances Series

Dancing on Broken Ankles

The Stars We See

A Heart that Dances

A Heart that Loves

Water and Stone Duet

Ruby in the Water

Lily in the Stone

Milton Keynes UK
Ingram Content Group UK Ltd.
UKHW052102300624
444882UK00004B/239